CW01431476

BROKEN GROUND

BROKEN GROUND

Uncertain Stories
Volume One

Edited by Rob Redman
Illustrated by Lucy Scott

Broken Ground

Uncertain Stories Volume One

First published in 2025 by Uncertain Stories Ltd.

10 9 8 7 6 5 4 3 2 1

This collection © Uncertain Stories Ltd.
Individual stories © their respective authors.
Artwork © Lucy Scott.

This book is sold subject to the condition that it shall not, by the way of trade or otherwise, be lent, resold, hired out, or otherwise circulated without the publisher's prior consent in any form of binding or cover other than that in which it is published and without a similar condition, including this condition, being imposed on the subsequent purchaser.

ISBN: 978-1-911757-00-9

The stories contained within this volume are works of fiction. Any resemblance between people or businesses depicted in these stories and those existing in the real world is entirely coincidental.

Uncertain Stories Ltd
3 Jamaica Street, Edinburgh, EH3 6HH, UK.
www.uncertainstories.com

Printed and bound in the UK by Gomer Press, Llandysul, UK.

EU Authorised Representative:
EAS Europe - Mustamäe tee 50, 10621 Tallinn, Estonia.

CONTENTS

INTRODUCING

BROKEN GROUND

ROB REDMAN

What are Uncertain Stories?

They're stories that take the world as it really is, more-or-less here, more-or-less now, and then they put a crack in that reality, just to see what light gets in.

They're stories written to grab you and pull you in. Because while we're increasingly encouraged — compelled, you might say — to waste our time on social media and doomscrolling and likes and one-more-episode streaming until it's suddenly two a.m. and that's another day gone, people sometimes forget that short stories exist, sometimes forget what they're worth as an art form and as entertainment.

But you won't forget these stories.

They come at you with their *what if* and *why* and *how* and *why not*, and in half an hour or less they've shown you a new world — or a new reflection of the one you thought you knew.

You could read a very short story like Shadow (p. 89) by Tamsin Hopkins, or Flo Ward's The End of the World (p. 109), in the time it takes to get a password reminder for your Tesco Clubcard account; you could spend thirty minutes scrolling through deeply unreliable gossip about an actor you've never actually seen in a film, or you could read Owen's

Wynd (p. 51), Eva Carson's salute to M R James, and find yourself feeling inspired to pick up some classic ghost stories, not to mention tracking down more of Eva Carson's own work (for which, watch this space).

You could spend the next half-hour adding shows to a streaming watchlist — shows which, in the end, will turn out to be okay, not bad, some good bits, the title sequence is quite slick, but the show itself is sort of a bit forgettable — or you could read The Builder (p. 13), after which you might well feel the need to treat yourself to a copy of David Frankel's collection of short stories, *Forgetting is How We Survive*.

In arguably less time than it takes to scroll through the extended introduction to an online recipe for fruit crumble, thumbing your way past sterile reminiscences of long-gone grandmothers, vaguely sinister targeted advertisements, and artfully composed overhead photographs of ingredients in little glass bowls, you could join the protagonist of Mark Taylor's All Seasons Sweet (p. 79), searching for the ghost of a peach and the real meaning of our relationship with food.

You might think that swiping your way through potential matches in a dating app is a better idea than reading What Remains of Us (p. 27) by Jack Edwards, but that's precisely and only because you haven't read it yet. And what could you possibly find on your socials that would fill a coffee break better than sitting down with Nathaniel Spain's What My Father Left Behind (p. 95)?

It's true of all of these stories: they're deliberate, and thoughtful, and engaging, and they're the product of human craft and human intelligence. Sometimes they're scary and sometimes they're funny and sometimes they're thought-provoking, and they're all worth your time.

It was inevitable, really, that when we sat down to put together our first anthology, we would find ourselves gathering a selection of stories with more than a hint of finality to them. This book starts with an ending, looks back several times over its shoulder (sometimes at the past, other times at something creeping along in the shadows), and ends in stasis. But really, it's all just a beginning. You can find out more about Uncertain Stories, who we are and what we're doing, on our website.

Just don't spend too long there: you've got stories to read.

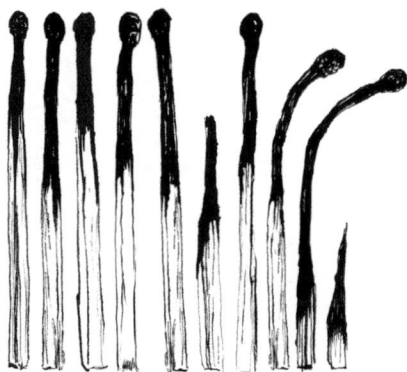

THE BUILDER
David Frankel

He's coming. Approaching via the old turnpike, across the hill — the old road. No one comes that way anymore, not on purpose. It's difficult to guess how far he's come, how long he's been walking; he is dressed as if for a long journey but he carries nothing with him.

At the boundary gate he stops, leaning on the post as though he's waiting for something, or maybe too tired to continue. He stands at the gate until the sun dips behind the ridge. The light dies first in the hollows where the stream cuts through the valley. Shadows collect in the cupped basins of dark water in the boggy fields, and under the short, bitter-leafed trees. They reach out from the folds of the dry stone walls, creeping outwards to join and spread along the steep hillsides.

When the shadow of the fell reaches him, he climbs the gate quickly, seemingly reminded of his purpose, and follows the track towards the house. The buildings seem at odds with their surroundings, misplaced. The house's heavy stillness seems separate from the motion of the trees and long grass around it, as though it exists in its own world, separate from the wind whipping at the land.

The main part of the house is made from cut grey stone, with tall windows and a wide front door. At one end of the main structure is an added wing, still old but roughly constructed of undressed stone. From it, small windows stare piggy-eyed across the back yard to a line of wooden sheds and an old stone byre. Beside them is a small garden where a rope that might once have been a child's swing hangs limply from a sycamore tree. His eyes linger on it for a moment as he hesitates briefly at the back door, before he turns the handle and pushes it open.

Inside, the kitchen is large, its walls lined with heavy, dark furniture, a table in the centre of its paved floor. The fireplace too is large, almost a room itself, with hearthstones polished by age, set into a deep nook. Its empty grate makes the room seem even colder. His familiarity with the room is betrayed by his lack of curiosity and the precision with which he locates the newspaper and kindling he needs to light a fire.

Before the last of the daylight is gone, he visits every room in the house, standing for a while in each one, looking around him. He allows his fingertips to idle on the objects sitting on shelves and tabletops, the clutter of domesticity, placed as though they have been recently set down, but coated in a fine layer of dust. The building is an engram of the people and the years that have passed through it. Every surface has marks: scratches on doorframes and furniture, scrapes on plaster and wallpaper, traces of movement; a hundred thousand minor events recorded.

There are a few dry logs in a wicker basket in the hearth, but that night he starts to burn things: books and small items of furniture. He sits by the hearth in the lurid firelight, sweating from the heat but still feeding the flames, and the air in the house seems to thicken, to slow, as though it is trying to push him out.

When the fire has died to embers, he climbs the stairs and enters the bedroom at the end of the landing. It is an ill-proportioned room whose high ceilings exaggerate its narrowness. The bed is unmade, its mattress bare, but there are blankets in the cupboard. The wallpaper is peppered with drawing-pin holes and stained by dots of Blu Tack. Lying in bed his fingers trace the outlines of the posters and photographs that were once there.

The day after his arrival he walks around the buildings, and circumnavigates the property's outer perimeter where lines of wire mark the bounds. On the other side of the wire, trees and a natural rampart of earth shield the house from its nearest neighbours down the valley. At intervals he pauses, looking back towards the house, weighing, considering.

The next morning, he rises early and begins to clear the rooms. Starting in the attic, and moving methodically downwards, the furniture is dragged out or cast from windows down into the yard where he piles the wooden carcasses and sets fire to them. Over the following days, tables and dressers are smashed and dragged to the yard and piled to wait for their turn in the flames. Wooden fittings — doors frames, skirting boards, picture rails — are crowbarred loose, broken down and fed to the fire. He finds a portable radio, switches it on, and for the first time in a long time, fragments of human voices sound in the house. When he throws it into the fire a moment later, its batteries burst with a bang, bleeding their chemicals and heavy metals back into the ground. The clothing he takes from wardrobes and drawers smokes the most. These most personal of things, some still holding the scent of the people who wore them, send a churning column of graphite grey up over the treetops, above the house, reaching for the rim of the valley.

Smaller timbers and splintered furniture are held back to warm the kitchen, where he has taken to sleeping, abandoning the bedroom, empty now. In the cold evenings, he tips out drawers — old letters, photographs, boardgames, placemats, clothes and toys, books and personal effects. Objects that have been well used, handled for years, treasured, and then half forgotten. They burn hot and fast.

The smaller pieces of furniture warm him for days. The dining room chairs are heavy, well built. It takes a lot of force to smash them against the stone floor, and they burn slowly as he feeds other, smaller stuff into the flames around them. The stained and ancient hessian runner from the hallway is carved into strips with a kitchen knife and stinks as it burns.

The fire burns more or less constantly, driving the cold from the emptying rooms. He pauses his work only to sleep and to eat indiscriminately from the well-stocked pantry — jam for breakfast, tinned pears for dinner. Every other day, he checks the postbox down by the road for letters confirming the closure of bank accounts, the settling of bills and cutting of services, the severing of ties. He registers their contents without expression and places them into the smouldering heap of embers in the yard where they blacken and flare.

Days pass and the inside of the house is cleared of furniture, joinery turned to embers; even the wallpaper, scraped easily from damp-dusted walls, is reduced to ash in the same fire that carried off the furniture and doors. As the furniture and ephemera of life vanish, emptiness forces its way in. He feels the pressure of it. The absence of the people who have slept and lived here hangs in the spaces where their things used to be, like a vibration in the air. The rooms should be empty

— should feel empty — but, in the corner of his eye, figures catch the light. He lets the scenes play out in his peripheral vision knowing that, should he turn to look directly, they will disappear.

As the house empties, he goes out to the sheds and takes out the tools he will need, before smashing the old wooden structures to the ground, dragging the broken sections into the centre of the yard and, with effort, setting the damp timbers alight.

While they burn, the stone byre is broken down, ancient mortar turning quickly to powder under the blows from chisels and sledgehammer. The roof timbers and door are dragged to the fire, which grows or diminishes according to the ebb and flow of his work. The fat old timbers smoulder for days, baking the earth to an ashy crust, and as they do, the byre walls are slowly beaten down to the level of the compacted earth on which they've stood for generations. When it's done, he stands on the bare ground, flashed orange by the light of the fire and the setting sun, and gazes at the house, its outline and black windows.

He shows no sign of remorse or sense of loss. All of this would happen anyway; what he has done is only an acceleration. It is not an act of destruction but a reformation — a fresh start, free from the archaeology of past events. There will be talk in the village, though. Even hidden behind its rampart of trees and banked earth, the unmaking of the house and column of smoke will have been glimpsed by the curious. There is nothing he can do about that.

* * *

A sledgehammer smashes through a wall, and sunlight burns a pale path across the floorboards. Before his eyes can adjust to the sudden change in light, he sees the figure of a girl standing in the corner of the room. It's the twitching of his lip that betrays his disquiet, but he looks away. It is a trick of the light — a shadow cast by the last curls of wallpaper hanging from the shattered plaster. The hammer swings again and again, for days it blasts light through walls, driving the shadows away until the upstairs rooms are gone and the ceilings are open to the cavernous web-hung lofts above, filling the house with the smell of shattered plaster and sawdust.

Standing on the joists, he begins to smash off the roof tiles. He hears them slither down the pitch of the roof, and the silence of their drop, before the slate smashes on the cobbles of the yard. One at a time they fall, until the house's ribcage is open to the sky. By noon he is sawing through the rafters, twisting them free, and allowing them to tumble down the outer walls and bounce awkwardly into the yard below. The old beams are the first really solid fuel the fire has had in days.

There is much that will not burn: pipes, cables, metal fittings, but eventually, even metal will rust and flake, staining the earth. Artefacts of iron or copper, dismantled, are buried. Not his tools, though — not yet, but their time will come.

The torches and lamps are gone now. When night falls, the only light comes from the fires in the kitchen and the yard, and shifting shadows claw the corners of the room as rainwater seeps down the broken plaster of the walls. The wind and rain have unfettered access to the interior now. As the elements enter, something else leaves, rising through the space between the chimney stacks and gable ends, and that night he feels unwatched for the first time since his arrival.

When he wakes, the weak sun is already filling the valley through a haze of fine rain that drifts like ectoplasm down the mountainside. How late is it? It is impossible to say: the clocks have all gone, even the slow-ticking grandfather that once stood in the hall. Their brass workings lie among the ashes of yesterday's fire, damp now from the drizzle.

He eats a perfunctory breakfast of tinned green beans, and stares from the window across the rubble-strewn ground where the garden had been, to the sycamore and its old rope swing. He finishes his meal and sends the tin clattering across the floor, before smashing the glass from the window and levering its frame loose with a crowbar. It falls clear and he pauses for a moment, looking out of the empty socket, before moving on to the other windows.

One storey at a time, the remaining walls of the house are smashed away, the masonry yielding to iron and slipping free. When he starts to demolish the back wall, he sees the castellation of broken stone echo almost exactly the outline of the hilltops of the ridge across the valley, as though the building is trying to trick him, to convince him that it is part of this landscape.

He uses the rubble to fill in the old well, rolling and shovelling spoil over the lip of the shaft, sending it down into the splashing darkness. The larger stones are used to block the narrow lane where it leaves the head of the valley road. He positions them carefully, extending the natural contour of the embankment across the track.

He loses track of how many days — weeks — he spends trudging to and fro, carrying stones, timbers, crunching smashed shards of roof tile underfoot and reducing the lawn and long-neglected flower beds to mud. The remaining stones — those he can carry — are taken to the scoop in the hillside from where they might have been quarried generations ago.

From the treeline his labour is watched, as though the shadows that his hammer blows have driven from the building have congregated in the spaces between the trees, longing to return, or to join him beside the bonfire. He doesn't see them, but senses them, a change in the air, a prickling of the skin, the hairs on his arm or neck bristling as though caught by the passing of a cold breeze. He pauses, listening for something other than the sound of his own breath straining under the labour of lifting and carrying. There is nothing. He returns to his work, scattering the stones from the walls along the sides of the track, and filling the ditches at the boundary.

His sledgehammer smashes through the flagstones and, for the first time in two centuries, sunshine falls on the soil beneath. He rolls the flags, end over end, to the bog pools in the valley bottom, where they slip beneath the surface, down into the soft depths. Once the flags have gone, the only paths remaining are desire lines of churned mud, and in time they will be lost under turf and bramble thicket.

At the boundary, he takes out fence posts, cutting the wire so it springs free and recoils like a wounded snake into the undergrowth. The land will fend for itself. The grass has already grown high, and thistles and other wildflowers in the fields and woodlands will invade and spread; trees too, one day.

The plastic pipe from the new bore-hole — the well's modern counterpart — is withdrawn like a needle from a vein and thrown onto the fire where it melts and bubbles into scorched treacle, fuming as it sinks into the ash. The brook will do for water. His shelter now is a makeshift construction of floorboards and rugs that stands where a few smashed hearthstones still mark the site of the old kitchen fireplace. The ground there is blackened and baked hard by the fire he maintains, feeding it from a diminishing pile of fuel.

Over the weeks of his great labour, he has changed. His body has grown leaner, his hair and beard longer. He looks tired, reduced, but he persists, until nothing of the house remains. And yet, even then, it seems to fill the space where it once stood, as though the idea of it can't be so easily unbuilt.

* * *

On a clear, cold morning when his task is almost complete, he wakes early and leaves the boundaries of the property for the first time since his arrival. Before the sun has cleared the hills and brought the village to life, he walks quickly down the ribbon of degraded tarmac that links the outlying farms. At the valley's open mouth is a clot of stone houses with a schoolhouse and a phone box glowing red in the grey dawn.

He walks past the houses and into the trees behind the schoolhouse, along the footpath to the reservoir beyond the village. When it forks, he turns right, climbing to a viewpoint overlooking the water, where he settles heavily onto a wooden bench. It seems as though he means to rest and watch the sunrise paint the waters of the reservoir gold. But instead, he looks down at the weathered timbers of the bench and traces the grain with his fingertips. Taking out a knife he digs away at the names scratched there, carving back the surface, curling away shavings of wood, until the names are gone. He wipes the indentation with his thumb to satisfy himself that the erasure is complete, then retraces his steps along the valley.

Back at the house, the end of the track itself is obscured now by banked rubble, but the old gate and postbox still mark its place. He fetches his tools and takes down the gate, then breaks the postbox free. Dragging them with difficulty over the debris-strewn ground, he throws them onto the piled embers of the fire, stirring up the ashes and encouraging the flames to take hold. As they rise again, he takes a bundle of documents and a leather wallet from his coat and throws them too into the fire. He watches them smoulder and then flare among the coals and ashes.

These documents are the last tangible proof that any of it was real. There are still lines of code in cyberspace, but data will expire or be deleted, or will linger on servers that will eventually fail as all things do.

* * *

The fires are gone now. There is nothing left to burn. Even his shelter is gone. The days are growing shorter and the wind funnelling along the valley is growing colder and more persistent, blowing the grit of crushed mortar and the ash from the fire across the boggy fields in a final act of dissolution.

At the head of the valley, along a path that is barely visible between heather and stones, is a small tarn, a circle of black water, surrounded on three sides by the last rocky curl of the scarp, like a borehole through the earth's cold mantle to the dark below. From its bank he throws his tools one by one into the water. As the last one sinks forever out of sight, and the ripples disperse and still, his lips move. He speaks for the first time since he came here, but the wind pouring through the valley carries his words away, and they are lost with everything else.

Beyond the tarn, a narrow path twists upwards into the hills. He climbs the path without looking back. As he disappears among a muddle of craggy peaks, heavy raindrops begin to fall, striking the ground like musket balls, filling the tread of his footprints in the churned soil where the house once stood, dissolving their outline until there is nothing left. But, beneath the sycamore in the scab of mud where the house's garden once lay, the remains of the old rope swing still hang, lank and rain-soaked, and as bright sunlight floods the valley again and birdsong fills the woods and fields, it begins to move.

WHAT REMAINS OF US
Jack Edwards

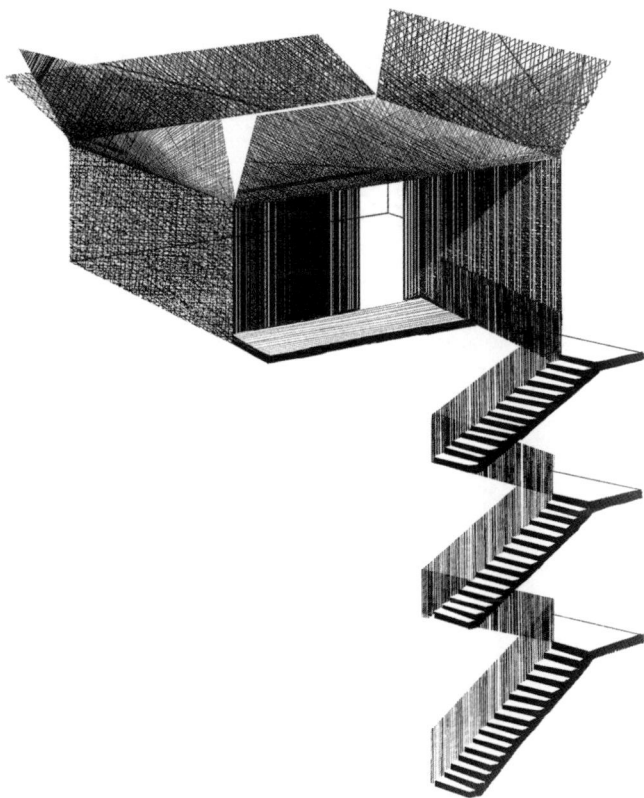

Eleanor shut herself inside the cubicle and stood there for a moment, rubbing her temples with the tips of her fingers.

Nathan had complimented her hair and offered a kiss on the cheek when they'd met at the pub earlier in the evening. A better start than most, but things had gone rapidly downhill from there. It was turning into a contender for the worst date of all time, in fact. She could leave now, slip from the toilet to the pub door without being seen. But then again, the apps and matches and chats and meet-ups were more for her own self-esteem than any honest attempt at finding love.

'Suck it up,' she said to the empty cubicle. 'New life, new you.'

She made her way back to the table, edging past an army of blokes in football shirts, crowded round a huge screen.

'Oh hey, there she is.' Nathan smiled. 'Thought you'd fallen in.'

Eleanor slid back into the seat opposite him. Frothy dregs lay at the bottom of his pint glass, a fresh one bubbling beside it.

'Not that I might have ditched you?'

He laughed, eyes lighting up. He was attractive underneath the flashy haircut and designer clothes.

She took a sip of her own half pint. It tasted bitter.

'Do you not like it?' he asked. 'I can get you something else.'

'It's fine, thanks.'

'A Coke or something?'

A deep, defiant swig. 'I'm fine.'

He nodded and cleared his throat. 'We were talking about my job.'

No, *he* was talking about his job.

'Mm,' Eleanor hummed.

'So, yeah, really it's nowhere near as exciting as in the movi —' A roaring cheer from the football crowd cut Nathan short. He glared down at the table, fingers dancing an erratic beat against the hard wood. 'Did you want to go somewhere else?'

'What's that?' She cupped a hand behind her ear, grinning. 'Can't quite hear you.' The footie fans were chanting and sloshing pint glasses above their heads.

Nathan drained his beer and the pair huddled out into the pouring rain, the city street a glistening river reflecting headlights and the fluorescent signs of bars and chip shops.

'Look.' Nathan leaned in. 'If this is too forward then that's totally fine, but my place is right around the corner.'

Eleanor shot him a look. The chancer. But the thought of another shouty city centre pub didn't appeal. And he seemed nice enough, if apocalyptically self-absorbed. She nodded her agreement.

He owned a basement flat in an upmarket area, the kind Eleanor found herself staring down into on the walk home from work. Clearly his boring job paid well. An abstract painting hung in the entrance hall, beside a neat coat rack and shoe shelf. He ushered her into a lounge adorned with more artwork, leather sofas, and a bookcase filled with volumes on finance and economics. He gestured to a drinks cabinet on the opposite wall and suggested Eleanor make herself something. She poured a gin and tonic as Nathan examined a row of aged whisky bottles, hoping she'd ask about them. She didn't, instead taking a seat on the sofa, eyeing a thick coffee table book she'd seen in the gift shop at the National Gallery.

He sat in an armchair, keeping a respectable distance. 'So, Ella, you just moved here?'

Something twisted in her chest. Her fingers curled. 'It's Eleanor.'

Only Christopher had called her Ella, and she'd not liked it even then.

Nathan bowed his head in contrition, 'Apologies.'

'Yeah.' Her voice wobbled, words sticking to her tongue. 'I've been here a few weeks…' She cleared her throat. 'Can I use your loo?'

She followed his directions down a snaking hallway, past a lavish kitchen and an office. She paused by the bathroom. A door at the end of the hall stood ajar. Eleanor pushed it open, the hinge squeaking lightly. Nathan's bedroom, looking a bit like a swanky hotel room, complete with solid oak furniture and a throw on the bed. He was the oldest young person she'd ever met. A row of ornaments were arrayed on the dresser, crude clay animals coated with a thick glaze. An elephant, an ox, a lizard, a zebra, and several others. Trinkets from the trek across Asia he'd been going on about? Eleanor picked up and examined the elephant, then slid it into the back pocket of her jeans. She flushed the unused toilet and ran the tap before heading back to Nathan.

'I'm not feeling too well,' she said, hovering by the door.

'Oh, okay.'

An awkward pause.

'I'm going to head off.'

He saw her out, looking confused by the sudden turn. She rejected his offer to escort her home.

'I'll text you,' she lied.

She took a bus across the city. Stone buildings loomed over the road from either side, stoic and unchanged as the city had shifted around them over the centuries, peering down at the Saturday night revellers quick-marching through the downpour or huddled beneath covered smoking areas, faces obscured in a cloudy haze of filtered tobacco and flavoured vapes.

Eleanor lived down a quiet side street. The area was nice enough, though rough around the edges. She'd emptied her savings account, everything she had left from before, and managed a deposit for a one-bedroom flat in an old tenement block. It'd been a quick sale, very little hassle, and a bit of a steal, despite the place needing plenty of work.

She bustled into the central stairwell, out of the rain. A dim bulb glowed orange on the lobby wall, casting long shadows across the tiled floor, highlighting a litany of chips and cracks. A large door at the back of the building lead out into a rear garden. It was broken, hanging half open as if it'd been kicked in, letting a cold breeze whistle through as rain pattered onto the tiles. She'd been meaning to canvass the other residents about getting it fixed.

Her footfalls echoed up into the yawning space of the stairwell, the tunnelled throat of some ancient creature, as she climbed the steps, passing the doorways to other properties.

Somewhere, muffled voices yelled at each other; there was a burst of raucous laughter from a flat below. She'd never actually *seen* any of her neighbours, but she heard them at all hours.

Her flat was silent, empty, a black void stretching into nothingness as she opened the door. She flicked the light on, its new unshaded bulb explosively bright, and hung her coat on the back of the door, letting it drip onto the rubber mat.

Ella. *Ella.*

Something ran the length of her spine. Christopher's voice an echoing memory, a recording she couldn't erase.

In the kitchen, she boiled the kettle and made a weak tea. The fridge hummed and creaked unhappily. She eyed the pale, drab walls with their peeling paint and the sickly water marks left over from a leaky pipe in the property's past life. The whole place was stagnant, decaying in comparison to Nathan's flat.

Above, someone yelled. Someone else responded.

She padded softly down the corridor towards the bedroom. *Her* bedroom, where she slept alone on a double mattress, wrapped up in a thick duvet, with only the sighing wind outside for company.

Sleep beckoned, but there was something else to do first. She turned and hovered for a moment outside another door in the corridor before inching it open.

The box room was a dank, windowless space which lay at the heart of the flat, an earthy whiff of something like damp rot lingering inside, with no airflow to whisk it away. It was empty, save for a cardboard box sat neatly at its centre, bound tightly with parcel tape, the words 'YOU'RE SHIT' scrawled on the side in black marker. Christopher had always struggled with that particular grammatical snag, though the unintended sentiment still stung.

Atop the box sat a scattering of random items: a lighter, a marble, this little plastic case shaped like a polo mint, two Pokémon cards (which said a lot about the type of guys she attracted), and some kind of half-chewed toy soldier thing. She added the clay elephant to the collection. Her collection. These were the things she'd gathered in her new life, replacing everything lost in the old.

Her past self was gone. It had no bearing over her future.

Eleanor sat by the box for a while, sipping her tea, humming an old pop song she'd forgotten the name of.

The sounds of the building and its other residents couldn't penetrate the box room.

In there, she was safe.

Outside lay danger.

And mistrust.

And confusion.

And heartache.

She drained the bitter dregs at the bottom of her mug, eyeing the box.

'YOU'RE SHIT'

* * *

'Please, sit.' Eleanor's line manager gestured to a chair across the table from him. He grunted as he sat, the seat hydraulics letting out a gasp.

She did as asked. They were in a small meeting room, its frosted glass turning the open plan office beyond into an abstract blur of colour and occasional movement, where dull voices droned as a phone rang and rang and rang.

'This is just a formality really,' he said. Lee was his name, though this was the first time they'd spoken beyond a quick hello in the break room. 'A catch up, see how you're settling in.'

Eleanor's hammering heart rate slowed. She hadn't done anything wrong. This wasn't a dressing down. 'Oh, well everything's fine, thanks.'

'Glad to hear it.' He laughed, pretending to close his notebook. 'Easy as that.'

Eleanor smiled. This would go quicker if she nodded politely and agreed with whatever he said.

'But really, that is good to hear.' He eyed her for a long moment. 'How was the first month then, out of ten?'

A five at best. 'Nine, easily.'

'Oh wow, things *have* gone well,' he smiled. 'I've collated some feedback from others on the team regarding your performance and just generally how you're fitting in.'

Eleanor's fingers curled beneath the desk, nails digging into the soft flesh of her palms. Keep it together. Smile. 'Oh yeah?'

'Mm,' he turned a page in his notebook. 'Fast learner. Has taken to the role quickly. Good phone manner.' Lee met her eyes, smiling softly. 'You get the idea.'

Another wave of relief.

'The only thing, and it's no big deal, totally understandable when you're brand new somewhere, but it's been said you're a little...' he searched for the word, 'standoffish?'

'Oh.'

'Maybe it's not that exactly. More like you're taking a little longer than some to find your feet on the team spirit side of things.'

What bloody 'team spirit'? She did what she was paid to do, answering phones and pinging out emails, and did it with a smile. What else was there?

'Well, I'm a little shy with new people sometimes.'

'Like I said,' Lee waved away her explanation, 'It's to be expected. You're new, still getting to grips with it all, the rest will come in time.'

Would it?

'Nothing to be worried about,' he finished.

'No, sure. I understand.'

'Good. You're a smart girl, Ella.'

'Eleanor.'

'Sorry, Eleanor. That's a long name,' he chortled, face blushing ever so slightly red with the exertion, 'Are you sure you don't prefer Ella?'

'I'm sure,' she smiled, nails threatening to break the skin of her palms.

She returned to her desk. Five emails had arrived in the brief time she'd been away. Her phone rang. She answered, eyes momentarily meeting Natasha's across the top of her monitor. Natasha gave a joyless smile, the expression confirming a blossoming assumption: Natasha had left the feedback. Or maybe it had been a whole group effort.

Team spirit.

* * *

She cooked a ready meal in the oven that night, picking at the molten mess of pasta and cheese while that pop song looped through her brain.

A booming knock at the front door sent a rattle through her bones. She hurried down the corridor and looked through the peephole. Nothing but the fish-eyed expanse of the stairwell beyond. She slid the chain lock into place and pulled the door open a few inches. Silent stillness.

'Hello?' Her voice echoed up and down the cavernous space.

No one answered.

Kids, probably.

A cold wind whistled up from the broken door in the hallway below. It needed sorting.

She went out onto the landing and knocked at her immediate neighbour's front door, but there was no response, just deep silence. It was the same at every flat on the floor below, save for one, a TV droning in its depths. But even there, no one answered her knock. She'd write a letter and post it on the empty noticeboard in the hall downstairs, maybe start a WhatsApp group.

A low moan echoed from somewhere above her in the stairwell, an eerie sound, as though something unknowable had turned its attention her way. She hurried back to her own flat, breathing a sigh of relief as the door clicked shut, then laughing at her own fear over the creaks and groans of an old building.

But the flat seemed suddenly gigantic, far too big for one young woman living alone.

A cold chill swept through the corridor. A pipe in the wall clattered and banged.

She shut herself in the box room, away from the noises outside, nestled in warm clothes, listening to music until the battery on her phone died.

* * *

'Wow!' Oscar beamed, kissing her delicately on each cheek as she arrived outside the restaurant. 'You look fantastic. I feel underdressed.' He looked down at his well-fitted jumper, the collar of a checked shirt peering out neatly above. His short hair was tidily swept to one side, and the five-o'clock shadow leant him a roguish charm.

Eleanor was wearing a new dress, something slightly flashy she'd picked up from a department store, a form-fitting black number which had looked great on the mannequin and almost as good in the changing room but felt somehow alien now. Still, getting out of her comfort zone was the important thing. Living her new life.

Oscar held the door open for her, a warm smile spread across his features. Inside, they were seated in a quiet corner, romantically lit by an ornate wall sconce and a flickering candle at the centre of the table. Their waiter, dressed in a waistcoat and bowtie, delicately placed a bible-sized wine list in front of Oscar and handed each of them a menu before gliding away.

'I'm definitely underdressed,' Oscar laughed. 'Didn't know this place was so fancy.'

Eleanor gave an embarrassed grimace. 'Me either. You honestly look great though.'

He smiled, looking relieved.

They ordered a bottle of the cheapest red and drew quiet contempt from the waiter when attempting to pronounce various items from the menu. Drink flowed, tiny plates of food splashed with streaks of colourful garnish were gawped at before being quickly cleaned, the atmosphere grew comfortable and familiar. They'd spoken briefly over the app, and that had seemed to be going well, but it was never clear whether something would click without meeting in person.

'You mentioned you've not lived in the city long,' Oscar said, munching on a dinner roll for sustenance. 'You're from around Manchester? Unless I'm really crap at English accents.'

Eleanor laughed, 'Well I'm bloody awful at Scottish ones.' She took a sip of wine as he grinned at her. He had a nice smile. 'But yeah, just outside of Manchester. Good ear.'

'I didn't want to assume,' he laughed. 'So, what brought you north of the border?'

For all the conversations she'd had since moving, no one had ever thought to ask that. There was no easy answer. 'I needed a change, y'know?'

He nodded, listening.

'I was with someone for a long time. Years.' She wrung her hands under the table. 'But I just kind of woke up one day and things were different.' She paused, gathering her thoughts. The feelings were easy to recall but difficult to relive.

'You don't have to go into it for my benefit.'

'No, it's okay. I think it would help.' Eleanor took another sip of wine, keeping the soft buzz of the alcohol alive in her system. 'I didn't know who I was anymore, or what I felt, what I wanted. We'd sort of… combined.' She raised her hands onto the table, lacing her fingers together in demonstration, 'I couldn't tell where he ended and I began. He was so strong minded, stubborn I guess. We did what he wanted, talked about things he liked. We socialised with his friends, whilst mine slowly drifted away.' Her throat wobbled.

Oscar's head tilted in sympathy. 'It's difficult, something like that. We give so much of ourselves to a relationship that it can all get blurred.'

'Exactly,' Eleanor nodded. There was nothing easy to point at, no fighting or cheating, just a numbness as she had slowly given herself away, piece by piece, love fading into resentment. They'd broken each other, then lived in their own shattered remains for longer than she could eventually bear.

Eleanor gathered herself, smiling softly. 'So, here I am. A fresh start.'

'I think that's very brave. Not many people can recognise a bad situation, let alone get themselves out of it.'

They turned down dessert, reasoning it would leave them wanting, and split the bill despite Oscar's insistence.

'Okay, how about this,' he said as they stepped back into the cold night air. 'There's an amazing ice cream place around the corner, my treat.' His enthusiasm was infectious. Everything about him seemed genuine.

'Or we grab a tub of Ben & Jerry's and head back to mine,' she countered, the words spilling out before she'd even realised what she was proposing. But he was nice and charming and sweet and had listened as she'd bared her soul. And the old her never would have invited a guy back after the first date, which was reason enough to give it a go. 'I'm not far.'

He eyed her. 'And you're not a serial killer, right? Because you should tell me now, so I have all the facts.'

'Not yet,' she said.

* * *

Ice cream in hand, Oscar followed her up the spiralling staircase to the flat, both snickering at a long and passionate moaning sound emanating from behind one of the other doors.

'I'd give you the tour,' she said as they got inside, 'but there's not much to see. When I said I'm starting over, I meant it.' She showed him into a decently sized front room, which had a tall lamp in one corner and a few cushions on the floor.

'See what you mean,' he nodded. 'You do own more than one spoon though, yeah?'

Eleanor gave him a playful slap on the arm as he followed her to the kitchen. 'Consider yourself lucky we have light. I was using candles for the first few nights because nowhere near here sells something as basic as bulbs.'

'That's city living for you. Impersonal and weird.'

They sat at the mismatched table and chairs she'd found at a charity shop, spooning softened mounds of gooey ice cream straight from the tub. They talked about movies and books and some of the nice walks to be had around the city. He suggested they go see a play in a few weeks. Butterflies danced in her stomach.

Oscar leaned back in his chair with a sigh, 'That's it, I'm stuffed.'

'Mm, same.' Eleanor slid the tub into the freezer.

He eyed his watch. He'd not checked his phone once the entire night, another point in his favour. 'It's getting late, I'll sort an Uber.'

'I mean,' Eleanor leant forward, biting her bottom lip, heart thumping in her chest, 'if you wanted to stay...'

His eyes lit up.

* * *

She awoke in darkness. The wind howled outside, sending a tin can rattling down the street. Except for several piles of clothes and a mattress on the floor, the room was empty. So was Oscar's side of the bed. She called his name softly into the dark, but there was no reply. Then she heard a soft murmuring out in the corridor.

Wrapping the sheet around her, Eleanor stepped lightly towards the door, a floorboard groaning underfoot. Somewhere in the depths of the building, a voice called out in a twisted mix of pain and pleasure before abruptly cutting out. She'd still not seen any of the other residents, but the haunted sounds that echoed around the building had begun to chip away at her sanity.

The main corridor of the flat was still and silent. A voice trailed through from the lounge. Oscar.

'I'm not having this conversation right now. I'll come see you later.'

Eleanor moved into the lounge and found the switch, light exploding into the space. Oscar, stood in his boxers, recoiled in horror, stabbing a finger at his phone then rubbing at his eyes as if he'd just woken up somewhere unexpected.

'Hey,' he said.

'What are you doing?'

'I just, um...' The pause to think was almost funny. 'Needed some water. Wandered in here by mistake.'

'Who were you talking to?' Her heart thumped at her ribcage.

'No one.'

She waited for the truth.

Oscar let out a long sigh. 'It's complicated.'

'Is it?'

'I'm still sorting a few things out with the ex.' He'd not mentioned an ex. 'But it's all over. I didn't tell you because she's, I dunno, kinda mental.'

Christopher had said the same thing about her, told their friends she was unstable instead of having the good grace to admit that imploding their relationship had been a joint effort.

She stared at Oscar, a stranger in her home.

She'd been so lonely. It had left her vulnerable, prone to a mistake like this. Like snared prey.

'I think you should go,' she said.

'What?' His feigned sleepy confusion was gone now.

'You should go.'

He moved to touch her but she shied away. 'El —'

'Please.'

He stared at her for a long moment before giving in.

'Fine.'

She followed him into the bedroom and hovered nearby, eyes averted whilst he dressed, despite having already seen him naked. He sidled past her, stopping for a moment to attempt another explanation before thinking better of it. She heard him slide his shoes on in the corridor then leave, gently closing the door behind him.

She clasped a hand to her mouth, holding back the sudden threat of tears. It was wrong. All of it. Men, work, the flat. She was a shell, an idea of a person, living a hollowed-out existence in a world of fleeting interactions.

Darkness seemed to move around her, unknown hands probing from the shadows.

She opened the shutters covering the bedroom window, sending a silvery finger of moonlight cutting across the floor. Something glinted, half hidden beneath the mattress. Oscar's watch. She handled it, turning it over, tracing a finger along the leather stitching of the strap, twisting the small dial on the side, sending the hands spinning back through time, wishing she could do the same. She'd do things differently. All of it.

The earthy, rotting smell of the box room had grown stronger. She placed the watch amongst the other trinkets, stolen shards of strangers' lives which she'd taken and claimed for herself, like Christopher had done with her, consuming her piece by piece.

This couldn't go on. She was falling apart.

A woman screamed out in the stairwell. A raised voice responded. The sound of a scuffle. Eleanor tore out of her flat in her nightshirt, barrelling into the rickety banister on the landing outside and glaring up and down. Silence. Emptiness. The orange bulb in the lobby below flickered. The wind moaned outside.

Shit. Shit shit shit.

The building was a nightmare of echoes and afterthoughts, like warped music playing from a half-chewed tape, her neighbours trapped like she was, broken and alone. All of them there, but not.

She needed help.

Eleanor retreated to her bedroom. She grabbed her phone and scrolled down the list of contacts, finding her mum's number. They'd not spoken in months. The clock in the corner of the screen read 02:19. Eleanor pressed the call icon and waited. And waited. And waited.

'Hello,' a robot voice answered, 'The number you have called is no longer —'

Eleanor hung up.

There was no one who could help. No one. She was alone. And it was all her fault, letting her friends and family drift away, connections rotting and falling apart. She'd said and done things that weren't like her. Had hurt people by pushing them away. All for him.

Him.

Christopher.

Maybe existing without him was no longer possible. He'd taken so much that she couldn't hold things together without him.

She found his name in her contacts. She'd kept it, some part deep down in her gut knowing she'd need it again.

The electronic trilling sang in her ear five times before someone answered.

'Er, hello?' A woman.

A woman.

Oh God.

'Is... Er. Christopher...?' Eleanor managed.

The woman huffed, 'Hang on.'

Eleanor hung up.

The floor dropped out below her. A crawling darkness swept from every rotten, fetid corner of the flat, rushing in to swallow her whole.

He'd moved on. Already. Eleanor was still picking around in the gutter just looking for half-decent conversation, and he was sharing a bed with someone comfortable enough to answer his phone.

She stumbled back into the box room, mind swimming, sweeping the collection of knick-knacks across the room before tearing into the cardboard and tape beneath. The words emblazoned on the side glared back: 'YOU'RE SHIT'.

Her shit. The last vestiges of a life outside of his influence. Remnants of her own being.

The top flaps of the box came away with a low growl as she savaged it open. The smell of death and decay blasted up from within. Eleanor recoiled, waving at the air. She kicked the box over, spilling the contents out across the floor: cookbooks, a small sewing kit, spools of coloured thread, a faded blue yoga mat, textbooks from the abandoned business degree, all of it scattered across the worn carpet, like the stomach contents of a disembowelled creature.

She stared at the detritus, leftovers of desperate attempts to know herself, to forge an identity separate from him.

Look where it had gotten her.

Something else lay amongst the waste. A dead mouse, rotting atop her belongings for months.

She bundled it all back into the box, rodent included, and hefted it down the staircase, winding around and around towards the ground floor. The building was silent. No one spoke or screamed or moaned or cried. She hummed that tune to herself, the one she couldn't quite remember the name of, as she traipsed back up the stairs, leaving the junk in the lobby for a moment and returning with a box of matches.

This would solve it. Would fix everything. Burn away the memories, excise every old version of herself, and maybe even cause enough of a fuss to finally bring her neighbours out into the light as flames licked and stalked the stairwell, creeping towards their eternally closed doors. Then she could start again properly. Reborn.

She struck a match and held it to the cardboard, eyes reflecting the flickering orange glow as the fire caught and the flames spread, leaping and playing over each other. A thick, caustic smoke billowed out and filled the space. She fell back, coughing and spluttering, watching it flow up into the stairwell. An alarm sounded, an ancient, broken, and twisted noise. But no one came to see. No one came, because there was no one there.

She was alone in the building, and always had been. The realisation clicked into place like a comfortable dream.

She watched the flames eat the cardboard and everything within, consuming the old her, burning it into a dark ash. The alarm stopped, perhaps the building itself having quietly flicked it off, sick of the noise.

Silence.

Peace.

* * *

Eleanor returned to the box room. The death smell was gone, purged from the space. She smiled at the scattered trinkets, picking up the clay elephant and rolling it around in her hands. She collapsed back against the wall and slid to the floor.

And then the voices came, calling out to her, some muffled, others as clear as if they were there in the room.

No fear now. Just warmth.

Darkness crept through the building, snaking along lonely corridors, creaking open old doors like it had countless times before.

Eleanor waited for its arrival. Waited for her new life to begin. Waited to be consumed all over again.

* * *

Oscar stepped onto the quiet street, spying the looming tenement up ahead. It had been a few days since he'd blown it. Should never have answered the bloody phone. Shouldn't have lied about it either, but he'd gotten flustered.

Idiot.

Eleanor had ghosted him, ignoring his apology, then the sheepish request to come pick up his watch. It'd been a gift from his grandad, nothing special, but sentimental. He'd just swing by, ask for it back and be on his way, no fuss.

The door to the block stood slightly ajar as he arrived. He pressed the buzzer for her flat. No response. Letting himself in could backfire, make a crappy situation even worse. He buzzed again. Nothing.

Oscar rocked back and forth on his heels. The street was dead, evening settling in across parked cars and rain-slicked cobbles. An empty packet of crisps gusted eerily along the pavement.

Fuck it. He just wanted the watch and he'd be out of her life forever. He stepped into the building, a shiver running through him as he entered the creepy, echoing stairwell. There was an odd smell in the air now too, as if something had been burning. And the back door was hanging off its hinges. The place was a bigger dive than he'd remembered. He climbed the stairs to her flat. That door too was open a crack.

'Hello?' he called.

No response.

The door sighed softly against the carpet as he nudged it open and stepped inside, calling again.

She wasn't at home. The flat was the same as when he'd last been there. He wandered, treading softly, checking the hollow living spaces devoid of furniture or life. Nothing. No one. And no watch.

He was on his way out again when he noticed another door in the hall by the bedroom. It opened with a long, low sigh into a windowless space.

Empty.

No, not quite. There were a few bits and bobs scattered across the floor: a lighter, a marble, some Pokémon cards, what might once have been a toy solider. And his watch.

He picked it up, wiped it on his jeans, and fastened it around his wrist, back where it belonged. The time was wildly wrong but otherwise it looked fine.

Should he write a note? He hadn't got a pen, and there was obviously no point looking for one, when the place barely had furniture. He'd text her to explain. Or maybe just leave it and move on. She'd stopped replying anyway, just another dead-end number. App-based dating was the *worst*.

As he stepped back onto the landing, a voice echoed down from somewhere in the building, humming some pop tune, the name of which escaped him.

A cold gust of air whispered through the flat as the tip-tapping of Oscar's feet on the tiled stairs grew steadily quieter, and the heavy door to the building slammed shut behind him.

Shadows danced in the darkness of the box room.

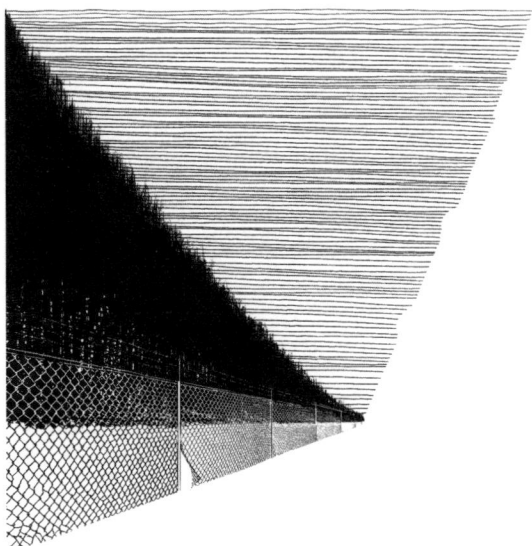

OWEN'S WYND
Eva Carson

As with shabby old manor houses, every proper marriage should have a ghost story in it. Mary and Steven found theirs in a village on the east coast of Fife.

The plan had been to go away for three nights with another couple they knew: Angela and Paul. Children were still a few years away, but careers had already crept in, so it had been a grown-up sort of booking, in the way that young professionals in their mid-twenties play at being grown up. There had been important talk about busy schedules and UK mini-breaks and picking somewhere nice.

Paul had found the hotel, in a quiet spot in Fife, and thought it looked like the sort of place the boys could go drinking and walking and fishing and the girls could — well, whatever they wanted. Mary had icily suggested that a city break would perhaps have been better. Angela had been less polite about it, and finally confrontational, and the day before the trip she and Paul cancelled altogether and looked to be about to break up.

This being the early 2000s, all of this was being relayed to Steven in a series of blocky and increasingly fragmented Nokia text messages from Paul.

'Just phone him,' Mary said.

'It's a non-starter,' Paul said to Steven when he called. Paul was in the early years of a career in finance, and his speech had become riddled with strange fragments from the office. 'Going forward, it doesn't have legs. But you can still go, yeah? It's fully paid. No refunds. Enjoy it for me, mate.'

Steven ended the call and dared to look at Mary. 'Are we going?'

'Yes,' Mary said. It was only a couple of hours from Glasgow, and already paid. And, she thought, they could always leave early if it was really dismal. Privately, she found herself more keen on the idea now that Angela and Paul weren't coming. Steven lifted their bags into the car.

Paul had, inexplicably, settled on a tiny Fife village called Wyndsgate. It was named for its wynds — wynd being pronounced like winding something up — but the village was pronounced 'Winsgate'. The word wynd was a kind of street name, meaning a narrow path off a main road. Wyndsgate had three unusually long, steep wynds that ran through it from the sea up to higher land. It lay in one of the little dents of beach and harbour that form the part of Fife known as the East Neuk. As well as its wynds, it had a handful of other streets strung out along the coast. And it had a single inn on the waterfront called The Creel, in which Mary and Steven were going to stay.

Paul had managed to get something right, at least: the rooms were big and had good views. When they let the front desk know that the other couple would not be arriving, the woman smiled and said she'd give them the biggest of the two reservations. The room she gave them was really two rooms: the door from the landing opened onto a sitting room that led to a bedroom.

Mary stood at the bay window in the sitting room. The walls were old and thick, and the windows had deep sills. It was mid-April, and the weather was sunny and clear. There were boats out at sea. To the right, just south of the harbour, was a high slope of the town with a small grey church at the top and a churchyard around it. To the left, north of the harbour, was the main body of the town. Beyond that was a wild promontory with a dense, shadowy forest stretching along it. The trees seemed gloomy, soaking up all the light, despite the high sun.

It was one o'clock. Mary realised she was hungry.

The bar presented them with macaroni cheese and chips, and they were given a table next to a large floor vase stuffed with dried flowers.

'Lovely,' Mary said.

'Give it a chance,' Steven said.

'Okay,' Mary said. 'But we'll have to go full tourist on it, then. Get a book or a leaflet. A map.'

Steven watched her to see if she was being sarcastic. He decided that she wasn't.

'We could go for a walk and see what we can find?' he said.

'Why not? There's the harbour. And I saw a little church. And did you notice the forest, further along the coast?'

There was an elderly woman in the bar, the only other person there, and at this she turned to look at them. Embarrassed, Steven and Mary realised they'd assumed she was hard of hearing because she was old. But she'd heard every word.

'I wouldn't go there, to the forest,' she said. She had an English accent. She was in her eighties at least. Her cardigan was knitted in ribbed white wool. Mary thought there was something beautiful about the way the patterned cuffs of the sleeves sat against the roped veins and textured skin of her hands.

'Is it private land?' Steven said.

'Something like that,' the woman said. 'It's all shut off now anyway. Stick to the main paths. Lots of nice things to see.'

'Are you staying over here too?' Mary said.

'That's right. Brought my two boys up here then went back to Suffolk. Visiting, now.' The old woman got up from the table and motioned to Mary to follow her. She made her way over to the fireplace at the other end of the room. There was a bookshelf there, built into the wall, full of handsome old clothbound books. The spines of the books were soft red, forest green, and pale yellow. In the light from the fire, letters in gold foil spelled out old names: Hodgson; Blackwood; M R James.

After a moment the woman pulled a thin yellow book from the shelves. She found the page she wanted, then walked back over with Mary to their table. She set the book carefully down beside Mary's plate.

Wyndsgate, North East Fife. *Owen Estate. Martin Owen, last living descendant, 1868-1901. It is well known that the Owen men practised magic, and that the estate was built by an ancestor over an ancient site from which it draws its power, and something walks there still. The estate and the Georgian sandstone property currently therein now derelict. Site receives boundary maintenance by the local council, who were left a considerable sum by the estate to ensure the land was never sold or disturbed. See:* **Wyndsgate, North East Fife. The Wynds**

Mary turned the pages. The book listed the three main wynds of Wyndsgate — Narrow, Church, and Owen's. Lots of Scottish towns, especially on the east coast, had wynds. The notable quality of Wyndsgate was the history, or myth, connected to its main three wynds and the name of the town. She looked at the cover of the book. *Eerie in the East: Scottish Ghost Stories Vol. 2.*

Legend had it that Wyndsgate sat on a very old spot, a kind of entry way to that part of Scotland by sea, and on its shore, men made the choice whether to turn to good, to convention, or to evil. Narrow, Church, or Owen's.

The old woman had been watching Mary read, looking over her shoulder at the pages. 'Enter ye in at the strait gate,' she said. 'For wide is the gate, and broad is the way, that leadeth to destruction, and many there be which go in thereat: because strait is the gate, and narrow is the way, which leadeth unto life, and few there be that find it.'

The woman had recited the Scripture comfortably from memory. Mary had been brought up in a Christian household and recognised it at once. Steven, on the other hand, only had a notion that the woman had said something Biblical, having been formed in a comfortably secular lower middle-class suburb. His relationship to religion went no further than the ragbag of hymns and services he'd been made to endure at school and at funerals, and the usual boy's navigation of the whole Glasgow deal with the football, in which he knew he was meant to regard himself as Protestant.

'Narrow isn't church?' Mary said.

'Narrow is much older than that,' the woman said. And it was as though she'd shot a bolt of strangeness through the picture bibles and Sunday school colouring books of Mary's childhood. The woman smiled.

'Well, anyway, we can go for a walk,' Steven said. He hadn't been rude, not exactly. Mary looked anxiously at the old woman, but her face was already set in an attitude of beatific wisdom. Or utter indifference. It was impossible to say.

'Thank you for this,' Mary said, lifting the book from the table. The woman raised her hand in acknowledgement.

'Enjoy your stay, lass,' she said. Steven frowned, and Mary nudged his shin with her foot under the table.

All three wynds were off the harbour road, barely a minute's walk from the front door of The Creel.

They soon found Church Wynd, with hanging baskets of pink and purple flowers at the doorways and bright fireworks of dandelions growing between the stones of the cobbled path. Church Wynd disappeared steeply off up the hill.

Then there was Narrow, and it maybe *was* a touch narrower than Church, but not by much. It was much plainer. As they passed it, some hikers spilled out of it onto the harbour road in sun hats and muddy boots.

And then, furthest north, was Owen's. At first glance, it was much like Church. There were baskets of flowers and prettily painted front doors. The cobbles were perhaps more uneven.

'We have to,' Steven said.

'I don't know,' Mary said.

'Ah, come on. The devil has all the best tunes.'

Mary followed him into the wynd. It climbed up the hill, past high white walls and dark front doors. They could hear seagulls shouting on the roofs. The cottages had burnt-orange roof tiles and the walls were coated in a thick white roughcast. Parts of it had flaked off and left damp sores in the masonry.

When the gulls fell silent there was a hush between the high walls of the buildings.

At the top of the hill, the wynd joined another road, which ran parallel to the harbour road. By a trick of geometry familiar to anyone who has tried to follow a trail along a coast, the wynd had performed some clever turn. They no longer had the sea at their backs; instead, there was the length of the town running south. They were facing north, towards the gloomy forest of the Owen estate high above them on the horizon.

'Hm. Not that spooky,' Steven said. Then he tutted and rolled his eyes. Mary knew at once that this was because of the man with the ball chucker. Across the road from the wynd, on a patch of grass behind a street sign and a grit bin, a middle-aged man was using the long-handled device — they were still quite new then — to throw a ball for a collie that was turning in rapturous circles at his feet.

Steven seemed to have some sort of idea about masculinity tied up in the opinion that people — men in particular — should just throw the ball for their bloody dogs. It was as though he'd secretly come from a line of proud all-star West of Scotland baseball pitchers and felt a good throwing arm to be the true measure of a man. Mary had discovered this particular aspect of his personality the year before, on a trip with Steven to Balloch.

Mary watched the collie race madly along the grass in pursuit of the ball.

Steven strode forward, where the road kept rising towards the forest. Mary didn't follow.

'Hey, I think I'll get you back at The Creel,' she said.

'Oh, come on,' he said, but he was still smiling. They hadn't quite fallen out yet.

'No, seriously. Have a good time.'

'Is this about that woman in the bar? The Bible stuff? Come on. Nonsense.'

She didn't say anything.

'You know what I mean,' Steven said. 'It's nonsense. Come on.'

'That's not how it felt to me. It's like a kind of home to me,' Mary heard herself say. And it was true: she hadn't thought much about church or Scripture for the longest time — and couldn't say she'd ever quite *believed* — but she'd grown up with all that. And the old woman had reminded her of it, and she didn't want to throw away the feeling it had given her by ignoring what she'd said.

There was a sudden, drawn-out, ear-splitting whistle. On the grass opposite them, the man with the ball chucker was looking anxiously along the road.

'He's away over the hill,' the man said. He put his fingers to his mouth and whistled again. Mary winced.

'Ah for God's sake,' the man said. 'He usually comes back. Whistle and he'll come for you. Wee bugger. Barney. Barney!'

He gave another piercing blast.

There was an agitation in the distance; it resolved itself into the shape of a collie hurtling towards them. The man's dog returned in a spray of mud and grass, and dropped a spit-soaked tennis ball on the ground. The man picked it up delicately with the chucker.

'You're honestly not coming?' Steven said.

Mary looked at her watch. It was two o'clock. 'I'll see you back at the hotel. No rush.'

'Honestly?' he said.

'I mean, I'd rather you didn't go either?'

'Why?'

She shook her head.

He laughed. 'I'll see you back at the hotel,' he said.

* * *

Steven began loping away up the hill. He was glad Mary had decided to turn back: it gave him a chance to work out his irritation through his legs. He was pissed off. He felt embarrassed about the whole trip, as though Paul had played some kind of trick on him. It would get turned into one of Paul's annoying funny stories, that Steven and Mary had gone to this random village and tried to have a holiday in it.

But he knew it was just Paul's usual nonsense: he always had these half-stewed plans and whims, and Steven always went along with them, because it was Paul and they'd known each other forever. Steven was annoyed at himself, really, for bothering to come. And a bit annoyed with Mary, who appeared to have been spooked by a superstitious eighty-year-old. And look at what she was missing: the views were already opening up on his right-hand side, as the road climbed, and the sea sparkled below. If there was a decent wee pub somewhere up here, he'd treat himself to a pint then tell her all about it.

He'd never been in Fife before. Well, Dunfermline once for the football but that didn't count. People said the east coast was a different world and it was true: all the wee cottages were different, and the place names, and way it was all set out by the sea like a picture on a biscuit tin. The west coast was more brutal, more windswept and industrial. As he thought this, he could feel the damp Glasgow weather in his bones, as though the city itself was in him. It was strange, he thought with all the profundity of a twenty-six-year-old: you could jump on a plane anywhere abroad and think nothing of it; but drive a couple of hours to another part of your country and it taught you something about where you were from.

The road made a turn to the right, along the promontory, but where he'd hoped to follow it all the way to the forest, it simply came to a stop. The tarmac ended at a grassy stretch of parkland — and look, there was another bloke who should know better, chucking a ball with one of those handle things. The forest was — what? Half a mile further on?

The trees were just as dark this close. It was like they didn't let the sun in under them. You could maybe see how local people started telling stories about a place like that.

You didn't have to believe them.

It was with a perverse sort of determination that Steven left the road and struck out toward the trees.

The middle-aged man with the ball chucker shouted after him.

'Nothing up there for you, lad,' he said. He had a strong Fife accent. A big black Labrador panted at his feet.

'Is it your land?' Steven said.

'No, no. You're surely no fae here or you'd ken no to bother. Are you after the coastal trail?'

'No,' Steven said. 'The forest. The Owen Estate?'

'I wouldn't bother,' he said. 'Braw day for the coastal trail.'

'I'm just going along for a look,' Steven said.

'I wouldn't,' the man said.

'Thanks, mate,' Steven said. He kept walking.

'Well, good luck with that,' the man said.

Steven didn't bother turning round.

As he approached the trees, he saw that they were behind a wire fence. Plastic KEEP OUT signs, the letters faded with age, were lashed to the fence with cable ties at regular intervals. He walked along the fence looking for a gap. As he walked, the left side of his body, towards the forest, felt colder — there seemed to be a chill coming from the trees.

He wondered if it was a local thing they were hiding, like folk drinking or taking drugs. He'd half been expecting to see lager cans and used condoms and needles in the grass. Scotland: Reality Edition. But nothing like that, or not yet. Then he found a spot where the wire fencing had come away from one of the concrete posts. He crouched down, prised it back further, and pushed himself through the gap into the estate. He decided his mission was to find the old house from the book. If it really existed.

The first thing he noticed was how quiet it was. He crossed the strip of uneven grass and entered the dense tangle of trees. There were overgrown paths — but they were still recognisably paths. As he walked along, other paths branched off, and it occurred to him it might be very easy to get lost. Feeling like a Boy Scout, he stopped, took two twigs, and crossed them over one another on the ground to help find his way back. As he was doing this, he looked up and saw a bird on the branch opposite him. A tiny bird, like a wren or a sparrow — Mary would know. But one of those birds that hops about constantly and is never still. Except this one was so still it looked as though it was frozen in place.

'Okay,' he said. The bird stayed exactly where it was. 'That's weird,' he said. He stood up. Only then did it hop away from him, and he felt an immense and stupid relief when it flew away.

He walked for ten minutes, fifteen, twenty. There was a sense, he had to admit, that something was moving through the trees — but low down — certainly nothing human. Deer, maybe. Or a dog. He walked on, crossing twigs on the path.

Then, he thought there might have been a noise — a very faint rasping noise, but with a mechanical-sounding part to it, or maybe rickety, like bones. Some sort of bird call, he supposed.

A few moments later he found a strip of thick cloth — rough, like burlap sacking — slumped across the path. It was tangled up in itself and was damp and mud stained, as though it had been dragged through the undergrowth.

There was something shiny nestled in it — he reached down. It was a medal, he thought. Gold, with red enamel on it. It had a symbol on it, like an eagle. Military probably. These things were collectable, weren't they? He put it in the back pocket of his jeans and stepped over the cloth.

Just past there, the path opened out, and he found the old Owen house in a clearing of the woods. It was tall and grey and symmetrical, a proper old Scottish country house, weathered and sullen. Its old windows reflected the dark mass of the trees. The stone of the house was overgrown with weeds, and trees had taken root on the sills and even on the roof, but it was still standing. He walked around the house and was startled to discover that the clearing opened onto the edge of the promontory and a view of the churning sea to the north. He hadn't realised how far he'd walked. Now the entire forest stood between him and the tiny village of Wyndsgate sitting on the coast further south.

Steven walked up to the front door of the house. He put his ear to the peeling wood. He heard nothing. But he suddenly had a sense of the whole house behind the door: the great big empty waiting space of it. He decided, abruptly, that he'd had enough. He walked smartly away from the house and back onto the forest path.

And it looked — just for a second — like there was a man lying on the path. But it was just the cloth — just the cloth! Except that, from this direction, the way it was all twisted up, it looked almost like someone lying on their side. The head was a cowled hood, with a dark blank hollow where the face should be. And there was a creased, fraying strip of cloth that seemed to reach up towards that cowled face, like a sleeve without a hand.

He forced himself to walk towards it, but the illusion of a man didn't break apart. Rather, the closer he got, the surer he was there was someone folded up inside it.

To get past it, he broke into a run and leapt rather than stepped over it — and when he became aware that he was still jogging along the path afterwards, not quite walking, he forced himself to slow down.

He refused to be a complete coward, so turned to look back along the path. The cloth was gone. Okay, so that was weird.

Best to keep walking.

He saw that some of the crossed twigs he'd left on the path had already been disturbed.

Really it would be more unusual, he told himself, if there *weren't* animals in a place like this — and there was a real sense of them, moving through the trees. Low down, trying to keep themselves invisible. Ah — yes — there. He got a glimpse of one when he turned and looked back — something tan-coloured moving low through the undergrowth.

At the fence, Steven squeezed himself back through the wire. A wind came up as he walked away. It seemed to rush out from underneath the trees before it died down. Well, thought Steven, the walking had made him sweat;

that was why it felt so cold on his skin and chilled him so badly.

He walked back down to The Creel. Wyndsgate, with its twinkling harbour and colourful flower baskets, seemed twice as pretty as before. He'd taken the Narrow Wynd down, but only, he told himself, because it would bring him out a touch closer to The Creel.

Mary was on the bed in her vest top and jeans when he went in. She was lying on top of the covers on her back, as neat as a doll in its house. The curtains were drawn, and her eyes were closed in a way that looked fragile to him, as though she might have a headache. But she sat up right away when he came in.

* * *

Mary looked at him. He'd brought the outdoors in with him, as her mother used to say. He smelled of sweat and forest and mud. Women stayed home and men went away, Mary thought. She'd been thinking about how the village was also a harbour, and how they must have sent all their men out to sea. They came back, if they came back at all, with the other places still on them, woven into the fabric of the clothes the women had sewn for them and the jumpers they'd knitted. Men went to war, and went sailing, and went fishing. And trespassed like idiots on horrible old estates.

'How was it?' she said.

'All right,' Steven said.

'Did you find it? Did you get in?'

'Yeah, yeah, I did.'

'Are you okay?'

'Course, why?'

'You just seem — worked up?'

'No, I'm fine.' He ran his hands through his hair, which made it stick up. 'I need a drink,' he said. 'I thought there would be a wee pub.'

'What was it like?'

'Oh, horrible,' Steven said. 'I mean — well, whatever. Just boring. Middle of nowhere.'

'Did you find the house?'

'Aye, it was — just falling apart. Just empty. I should've taken a photo.'

'It doesn't matter,' Mary said. 'Anyway, there's a boat trip we can go on tomorrow. I asked at the desk. And there are shops where I might get something nice for Mum. That sort of thing. I don't mind it here, actually.'

'How perfectly lovely,' Steven said. He sat down on the bed and stood up immediately when she shoved him away with her foot and told him to get changed out of his muddy jeans.

They went down to the bar. There was a couple there this time, who had a small boy with them, maybe six years old. The boy turned in his chair and gave them a sticky wave.

Mary went to the bookshelves again and brought back the yellow book the old woman had shown her — and another one, thicker, which was a dusty red colour.

'The girl at reception said I could borrow them for the room while we're here,' she said.

'Cheerful bedtime reading,' Steven said.

'What's wrong?'

'Nothing — just, horrible stuff, isn't it?'

'I think it's interesting.'

'I'll get you a *Cosmopolitan* at the wee corner shop.'

'Ha,' she said. But he did look ruffled. 'Are you being serious?'

'No,' he said. 'Just ignore me.'

'Did something bother you up there?'

'No, honestly.'

'I'd visions of you being chased by local teenagers or something.'

'Not a soul,' he said.

* * *

Later, after a few drinks and dinner, they discovered there was a band on in the bar — folk music, old men in cardigans, ironic enjoyment — and after the band, they went upstairs. Steven saw that Mary had brought the books with her. He watched her put them down carefully on the side table by the phone in the sitting room. He followed her into the bedroom.

At three o'clock in the morning he woke uneasily. It felt as though, underneath the lazy fun of the evening, he'd been stupid enough to forget something important — like turning the oven off or locking the car doors. He sat up in the bed, then went into the sitting room. The curtains were open. There were lights from the boats out at sea, and moonlight trembled on the surface of the water.

None of the windows in the Owen house had been broken, he realised. The thick, warped glass. The way it reflected the dark trees. That was weird. In most places it was almost like an ancient tradition, for local kids to throw stones at that sort of thing.

Then he remembered something else: the medal. He drew the curtains and switched on a table lamp. The medal was in the back pocket of his jeans, and his jeans were on top of the suitcase on the floor. He pulled the medal out and sat down next to the lamp. It was circular and no bigger than a fifty pence piece. There was a square loop at the top for a ribbon to be fastened to it. It seemed to be made of gold, and the thing he'd thought was an eagle was something else — it had wings, but it also had four legs, like a lion, and its long face in profile had a muzzle, not a beak. The details were picked out in red enamel. There was a tiny red stone set into the metal for the eye. He thought it might be worth something. Maybe it wasn't a medal, in the military sense — but it was obviously something significant. He could look into it in the morning — or take it to an antiques shop in Glasgow.

He slipped it inside the suitcase and went back to bed.

And it was here that he began to have trouble with his dreams. As soon as he closed his eyes, there was a sense of something — something wrong. Something that had been waiting, poised, for his vision to be plunged into darkness.

The trouble was he was in the forest, there was no doubt about that. He was back there — with the thing moving in the trees, and having to walk quickly on the path to get away from it, back to the fence. But this time when he turned to look back along the path, the figure was there. It was crouching down in the dirt. Its face was hidden under the cowl of the mud-stained sackcloth. Its empty sleeves were clutched up by its sides. It began to rush towards him, moving close to the ground, like a man scurrying forward in a low tunnel.

He woke with a strangled shout. Mary muttered in her sleep. She lifted her head. 'What is it? What's wrong?'

'Nothing,' he said. He held her until her breathing slowed again and she was fast asleep. He tried, periodically, to close his own eyes, but the feeling of something waiting came over him again so that he opened them at once.

Early daylight was leaking in through the bedroom curtains when sleep overtook him; only then did he drift off. He woke with Mary gently trying to shake him out of it.

* * *

Mary told him that the boat trip was at ten o'clock. It was another bright, blue-sky day. They'd need to wrap up warm for the boat, but otherwise the weather was perfect. Steven followed Mary out onto the pavement. The elderly woman they'd met in the bar followed them out with a small suitcase.

'Safe journey,' Mary said to her, and the woman smiled. But something had caught the woman's eye — they followed her line of vision as she looked up at the front wall of The Creel. There was a faint but unmistakable trail of mud, maybe two feet wide, from the ground up to a first-floor windowsill. The window, Mary realised, of their sitting room. The woman looked at Steven.

It was a jaded sort of look, as though he were about to become a statistic.

'What?' Steven said.

The woman ignored him. 'Do your best to enjoy your trip,' she said to Mary. A taxi pulled up, its engine rattling. The driver was out at once, helping the woman with her suitcase. Mary waved her goodbye, then she and Steven walked down to the boats at the harbour.

* * *

The boat trip, on which they were the youngest passengers by about thirty years, involved heading out to a small rock of an island beyond the bay, turning a broad circle around it while being told about its seabirds, then heading back towards the shore.

'That's odd, isn't it?' Mary eventually said. The tour guide had just finished talking about the mating habits of gannets. 'About our window, I mean.'

From the boat, The Creel was just a tiny little square among the other tiny squares of the harbour. From this distance, you could see there was something in the idea of there being three routes in Wyndsgate: there must be something geological about it, Steven thought. The sandy harbour and main town were of one character; the gentle, loamy slopes to the south with the church land were another; and the dark promontory of the Owen estate was another again. It must have come from the sailors coming back in, this idea of the three ways.

'It's superstition,' Steven said. 'She's just a superstitious old woman.'

'That's not very nice,' Mary said.

'No, come on,' Steven said. 'You're spooked. But it's ghosts you're talking about. Evil and spirits. It's a lot of nonsense.'

'Something's bothered you,' Mary said.

'No, it hasn't. I'm just tired of it all.'

He really was tired; he hadn't slept well. He was sure all the talk from the old woman and Mary was why he'd been spooked. They'd sent him up there with his head full of nonsense.

Back on shore, they went for a walk along the harbour, and found the little shops Mary had mentioned wanting to see. He trailed behind her, yawning and trying to stay awake. They had lunch in a café, and went back to The Creel just before dinner.

The couple with the six-year-old boy were standing at the reception. The mother hesitated when she saw them and shot her husband an anxious look. The husband nodded.

'I'm sorry about this,' the woman said. 'It's a bit awkward. But are you staying here any longer?'

'Yes,' Mary said. 'Another two nights.'

'Well, it's just that my son happened to see inside your room earlier. When the maids were in. And it gave him a terrible fright. We were just wondering if you could move it from view of the door.' She looked down at her little boy. 'The — well, I imagine he's seen a kind of sculpture, is that it?'

'It was a horrible man on the floor,' the little boy said. 'A horrible man!' He turned abruptly red and began to wail. His father scooped him up.

'I am sorry,' the woman said. 'It's just — they were cleaning your room, and the door was propped open, and he happened to see it. Would you mind?'

'Of course not,' Steven said, 'So, I just — a sculpture?'

'We'll move it,' Mary said, smiling. 'I'm so sorry.'

'Oh, thank you,' the woman said. 'I do appreciate it.'

Steven watched as Mary went around their little sitting room systematically. She steeled herself and looked under each armchair. Then she did the same in the bedroom, even looking under the bed. She stood up.

'Why would it come in here?' she said.

'Why would what come in here?' Steven said.

Well, that led to an uneasy silence. Most people would have backed down — but not Mary. And certainly not Mary with Steven.

'You know what I mean,' she said.

To Steven, just then, her voice seemed to have become very tidy and neat and — yes, religious, somehow. She was her parents' daughter.

'No, I don't,' he said. 'I don't know what you mean.'

She frowned.

'I don't,' he said.

She looked disappointed in him. Steven suppressed an urge to yell in frustration. The books from downstairs, old and faded, were lying on the side table by the phone. He realised he'd lost patience with the whole thing: this stupid little corner of Scotland, this creaky old hotel, those stupid books! You wouldn't get ten pence for them at a car boot sale!

Mary went to the window in the sitting room and opened it. Faintly, across the middle of the sill, was a scrape of mud.

'The cleaners must have opened it when they were in,' Steven said.

'Well, yes,' Mary said. 'But then scraped mud over it?'

Steven said nothing.

'What did you do when you were up there?' Mary said. 'Did you disturb anything? Take anything?'

'No,' Steven said. But she was watching him. She could always tell when he was lying.

They ate dinner in the bar in silence. She'd brought one of the books back down with her and had propped it up on the table to turn the pages while she ate. The red one. It was a local history book. *Notable Persons*.

Neither of them wanted to mention the possibility of going home. Mary, because Steven had refused to acknowledge what she meant about the Owen estate, and Steven because he refused to admit anything was wrong.

Because nothing was wrong! It was just a spooky, crusty old place, and that wee boy just had an imagination — it would have been something the cleaners had in with them: bags of rubbish or crumpled linen lying on the floor. A horrible man! Nonsense!

They went back to the room after some music in the bar. Mary, Steven saw, had taken the Gideon Bible out of the bedside drawer and laid it on the table beside her head.

He lay next to her and tried to summon the courage he needed to close his eyes. But it was as though the forest was behind them — the dark of his closed lids was the heavy dark green of the trees. Ridiculous. It grew late and he gave up trying.

He went into the sitting room. The weather had turned, and the wind was throwing rain against the windows. He picked up one of the stupid old books from the bar and settled down in an armchair. He'd picked up the red book, the one about *Notable Persons* that Mary had been reading over dinner.

> **Martin Owen 1868-1901.** *Last descendant of the Owen family of Owen House (property situated on the promontory beyond Wyndsgate, Georgian with traces of older structures and habitation on the site).*
>
> *Found dead in the grounds of the estate aged forty-two, cause of death recorded as heart failure. Body discovered by a debt collector who had reluctantly entered the estate grounds to pursue the matter of an unpaid bill.*
>
> *Officially a family of textile merchants, using the harbour at Wyndsgate heavily in the eighteenth and early nineteenth centuries for trade by sea, though becoming steadily more*

reclusive until at the time of the death of Martin Owen they ran no business through the harbour at all.

Several of the men of the Owen family have been noted to be involved in occult activity, with local rumours reaching several generations back and with possible connections to business of such nature at Balwearie further down the coast of Fife.

They are thought to have carried out such activities under a corrupted version of the official family seal. The official seal shows an osprey above the motto 'No Greater Prosperity'. The occult seal shows a demon figure with similarity to the osprey in profile and the same motto. The occult seal of the Owen family of Fife has been found in correspondence over the past three centuries among European occult circles, most usually in connection with the pursuit of omnipotence through demonic power.

There were drawings of both the official seal and the occult seal printed in the book. Steven recognised the occult seal at once.

Just then there was a cold air that blew across the room, low down on the floor, and a noise: a faint rasping noise, with a rickety sound in it like bones. From beneath the empty armchair opposite him, the darkness of the floor drew itself together.

Steven watched it form into a terrible figure crouching on the carpet, the figure of a man, head wrapped in a cowl. Hardly in control of himself, Steven was out of his chair and falling into the corner of the room furthest away from it. But it rushed towards him, staying low to the floor, and when it reached him, it reared up. It gasped, and its gasp was the sound of air being drawn to long-dead lungs. The face — Steven does not, to this day, like to talk about the face — the face was made of the darkness inside the cowl. It was making a terrible, unspeakable noise. Steven screamed. He only knew that if the darkness touched him, he was finished. There was a fate worse than death there, if the darkness touched him, and he would have climbed the walls or leapt from the window to avoid it.

It was Mary that solved the matter. She'd come running into the room because of Steven's scream. She saw the heavy cloth hanging over him and pressing towards him. She screamed.

When Mary screamed, the thing fell to the floor and something seemed to pass out of it — some darkness seemed to scurry away along the walls. And then it was just the two of them — Steven, bent horribly into the corner of the room, and Mary. It was as though the thing had required utter secrecy to act: as soon as there was someone else as witness, its power fell away.

All the screaming had caused voices in the hall outside — Mary opened the door and found two anxious night staff peering in to see if everything was okay.

They'd just had a bit of a fright, Mary explained. False alarm. They'd thought something had come into the room, but nothing seemed to be there. Could it have been the weather and the old windows making a noise?

The staff were sorry to hear it and asked if there was anything they could do. Yes, actually, Mary said. If they could have the fire kindled in the lounge, and a stiff drink? Would that be too much? Well, not at all. And that was how Mary got rid of it, the wrap of muddy cloth that had fallen to the floor: a strip at a time into the fire, with Steven nursing a whisky and watching her and wondering who it was he had married.

The medal was returned to the Owen estate in the first light of the morning, by way of a ball chucker borrowed from an affable man walking his Jack Russell terrier on the last road before the forest. Mary kept the engine of the car idling while Steven walked solemnly out towards the trees, right up to the fence. He put the medal carefully into the cup of the chucker, then fired it across the top of the wire.

There wasn't much more to be said; they drove home. Steven admitted, about an hour into the drive, that Mary had been right. She knew he meant about everything, and especially about what he'd called superstition.

He worried, for a while, that the fright had altered him in some way — that his heart might have suffered, or his hair might soon turn white. But months, then years passed, and those worries faded away. If, even now, he goes pale at seeing a certain kind of dark, dense forest on the horizon, or halts at the sight of old cloth or tarpaulin on a walking trail, then that's only understandable. And if he's been more likely ever since to accompany Mary to church on occasion, and even offer up a few words of praise himself, then that's hardly surprising either, and very pleasing to Mary.

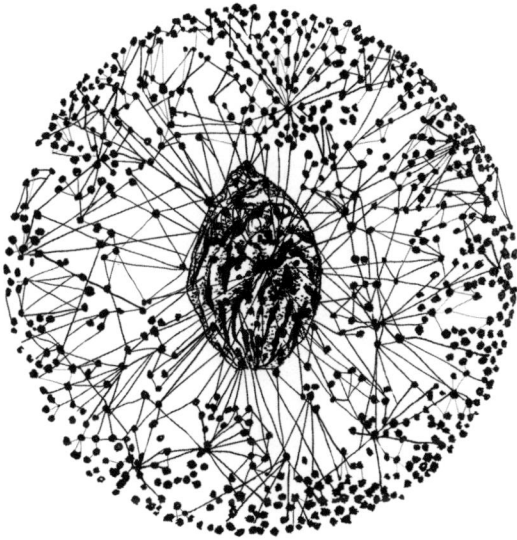

ALL SEASONS SWEET
Mark Taylor

Peaches came in a hundred engineered varieties, each insipidly perfect.

There were the big brands, a dozen names with three or four lines each, all vying for the same profitable middle ground of flavour. There were the specialist makes, for customers with refined tastes or acidic peach salsa recipes or a desire to seem unusual, all ultimately owned by the same two omninationals as the market leaders. There were the indie synths, crowdfunded on the promise of bringing back that real peach taste you remember, with pitch videos showing gorgeous juice dribbling in gorgeous rivulets down gorgeous chins, and long blog posts about the benefits of including the pit. The few indies that made it to market rarely reached a second crop. Those that did, sustained by sunk-cost-chasing backers who kept insisting they could taste the difference, grew until they caught the acquisitive attentions of an omni. Once the buyout became official the backers would drift, betrayed, to a new small-batch strawberry line. Rarest of all, there were the custom synth services, preserve (and conserve) of high-end restaurants, the ultra-rich, and the occasional enthusiasts' group buy, which tweaked everything from moisture level to fuzz length so you could be disappointed just the way you liked it.

Leo had spat out his first peach at the age of two and thought he would never look back — until, at the mid-March wedding breakfast of mutual friends, he was seated next to Amelia. When the beetroot salad was served, she was an acquaintance, seen across the pub at birthday drinks but hardly noticed. By the time of her monologue about the intolerable artificiality of the peach Melba, her obsessions were his obsession. He caught the bouquet and presented her with the single naturally grown rose from its centre.

Since then, he had tasted every peach on the market. The ones that impressed him, he tried out on her. Ignorant but enthusiastic, he bought gold-ribboned punnets for her to dismiss, untasted, as waxy. As the years went on, he joined crowdfunders and group buys and paid kitchen staff to smuggle private lines out of triple-starred restaurants. As his palate developed he brought fewer and fewer peaches back to Amelia, rejecting them in the terms she had taught him: too floral, too apricot, too fungicidal. On each anniversary, he presented his Peach of the Year, served to highlight its truest qualities, and together they dissected exactly how it failed. But by now, it was for tradition alone: like her, Leo had lost all hope in synthetic peaches.

* * *

In the afternoons, Leo liked to walk in the wildlands: those great gifts to the nation, the quid pro quo for the miles of monoculture that fed the synth works. Unofficial but well-worn paths marked the most popular routes: the scenic cut-throughs between housing zones, and the ways to waterfalls and glades and pools. On harder days, when it was wet or he was tired, he stayed on these paths, enjoying the easy walking and the rustle of wildlife. But when he had the energy, he stepped off, picking his way through wherever was passable, allowing himself to get hopelessly lost. He loved the smells of the meadows and forests, which only really came out when you trod your own path. He kept his phone off until he needed to navigate back to the gate. As a child, he had loved to spin blindfold until a room lost all familiarity. A wander in the wildlands gave him that same feeling. Amelia, preferring hills and sheep, stayed home.

It was on one of these walks, when he had slept well and the sun was bright but not hot, that he found the tree. He had seen enough in pictures (always alongside disclaimers: *synthesized product, does not represent actual growing conditions*) to believe that he recognised it. But everything looked different in the wildlands. He plucked a few leaves, took them home, crushed them between his fingertips and compared the scent against descriptions in old spotter's guides archived online. He returned four days in a row, once in driving rain: among the hard edges of the flat he could never quite trust his memory. He checked and consulted and thought and looked and smelled and tasted until he was certain, determined that he would not ask Amelia.

He restrained himself from going back more than weekly in case it dulled the pleasure. He knew the tree wouldn't fruit for months; he knew it would still be there, felling and clearing being prohibited in the wildlands and disease being much reduced. But he sat by it, touched its bark, caressed its leaves, and felt the fizz of anticipation. He knew that feeling from parcel deliveries and approaching holidays and that certain smile as Amelia walked towards him. He hadn't known that nature could provide it.

As the peaches swelled, he felt a smudge of disappointment, like the first scratch on the face of a new watch. There were so few of them. In the pictures, every branch had been laden, like a Christmas tree baubled by an unattended child. Here, the fruit grew in a few small clusters, which Leo struggled to pick out among the foliage. This, he supposed, was why humanity had moved on to synthesis, which was reliable, plentiful. But Leo would have sat there all year for a single natural-grown peach.

A fortnight later, they were gone, and Leo fancied the squirrels looked unusually pleased with themselves. A few tooth-scored stones lay on the underbrush: he pocketed them, wondering how long a peach tree took to grow from seed, and whether he could scrape together enough good earth to sustain it. At first, he had been sure he was devastated, enraged, ready to tear the tree out by the root and shoot all the squirrels. But he found that he wasn't. Synthesis was easy: this was supposed to be difficult. That was the point. To draw out bounties from the cold earth. By the sweat of his brow. A year wasn't such a long time.

* * *

Halfway to the tree, he wondered whether the paintbrush in his pocket was legal. The wildlands were, by law, wholly unmanaged: even at the gates, the paths would overgrow without footfall. As a national resource, access for all was guaranteed, and there was a general understanding that some degree of foraging was permitted. But Leo wasn't clear on the legal particulars, and hand-pollination seemed troublingly like interference. On the other hand, it was nothing more than the insects might chance to do. And didn't insects favour certain blooms, returning to them daily? The ones that were sweetest, or most colourful? They would bite holes in flowers to drink nectar from plants adapted to some other pollinator. He had read that somewhere, back when such things were just interesting trivia. The line between animal instinct and human ingenuity was a blurry one, everywhere except a wildland boundary fence.

Leo had kept up his weekly visits through autumn and winter, waiting patiently for the blossom. There was nothing to do until it came, but still he visited. Even when he set out to lose himself as he used to, he circled back this way. Not only for the joy of it. The wildlands were always changing, and when it was wet or warm or stormy they could transform themselves overnight. Waiting a month might leave the route unrecognisable. He had saved the location, of course; but somehow it was hard to believe that the coordinates on his phone mapped onto the landscape so neatly, that the wildlands could be navigated by tools other than their own. Now he understood that the magical forests in fairy tales and fantasy stories were not inventions, but exaggerations of the way the world really was.

As he touched the bristles of the paintbrush from flower to flower and worried about the law of the land, he thought about the squirrels. After they stole Amelia's peaches, Leo had started watching them, testing them, working out how they could be kept away when the next crop came. They were clever, even creative. But like every other creature in the wildlands, their cleverness was honest and direct. They did not try to understand what they could not directly observe. They did not, like Leo with his little paintbrush and his digitised gardening manuals, operate on faith. They did not know they were in the wildlands, and it was that which kept the wildlands balanced. Leo felt himself the grit in the machine, and he wanted it to be free of him. But not until Amelia had her peaches.

When the fruits began to show, he dabbed synthetic capsaicin around them to put the squirrels off. He was visiting every day he could now. When he didn't, he found he couldn't sleep for impotent worry. Deciding the capsaicin would not be enough, he cut up an old waste-paper basket to make a baffle for the trunk. It felt strange to be making things with his hands. Even as he struggled through the bioplastic with his kitchen scissors, he felt powerful. He tied strips of foil to the branches to frighten away birds. He looped netting over half of the setting clusters, unsure whether it would do more harm than good. He hesitated with a breadknife in his hand before laboriously pruning back neighbouring branches to beyond squirrel-jumping distance.

Now it really did look like a Christmas tree, hung all over with manmade decorations and carved into its own patch of sky. He kept his visits short now, and sometimes only looked from a distance, afraid to be seen. One wet day he found the low-hanging foil had been picked: someone had tried to tidy up. The baffle was askew where they had given up on removing it. A lone squirrel sat smugly in the tree's upper branches; Leo flung pebbles until it streaked red down the trunk and rustled away into the wildflowers. New growth was pushing out of the trimmed branches, like reaching hands. But the work was done, and the fruits were coming.

* * *

He took his first crop on a hot July afternoon. (It had been torture to present that year's anniversary peach, knowing it was a diversion and fearing she would love it.) Synth peaches were always perfectly ripe, so he knew what he was looking for: that scent from the fuzzy skin; that slight give in the flesh that warns you to be delicate. These peaches were smaller than he was used to, and yellower. If he hadn't checked up close, he would have thought them unready. But there were a few windfalls already, and the ripest on the tree gave only the lightest resistance when picked, like he was lifting his phone from its magnetic dock.

He had expected to take only a few today. Just those that had ripened quickest. Tomorrow, he would persuade Amelia to join him down the path he had worn, casually handing her a real, natural-grown peach as they drew near. 'Not just natural,' he would say as the tree came into view. 'Wild.' But it seemed half the tree was ready to fall: if he waited, he would be walking her to rotting windfalls and squirrels drunk on fermenting flesh. He filled his small backpack as carefully as he could, leaving his sunblock and spare socks and tea flask in the branches to make room. The baffle and the foil and the netting would have to come down later. The fruits that bruised would have to be cooked. Or canned for winter: what a thought.

As he began walking home, Leo tasted his first real peach, and knew instantly that Amelia would not like them. He had prepared himself for sourness and astringency. He had imagined that first bite as a challenge, nature saying to him: 'This is what the real world tastes like. If you want to enjoy it, you have to put up a fight.' Instead, it was thin and flavourless: not juicy, but wet; not soft, but slimy. The sweetest thing a wildland squirrel had ever eaten, but to

Leo it tasted like the synthesizer had glitched. And dark and hard and bitter at the centre of it was an unmistakable message that made him suck the flesh from the stone and reach for another: 'This was not made for you.'

SHADOW
Tamsin Hopkins

Jon is first aware of the shadow growing stronger on Thursday morning, when he lifts his coffee cup and sees another hand doing the same. The shadow hand becomes heavier as it holds his cup steady for Clare to give him a refill, the same way his fleshy hand does. He doesn't remember usually having a shadow this early in the mornings, but maybe he's wrong. Shadows are everywhere. If you look at your hand on the page, depending where the light is, there will be a shadow.

Jon sits on the bus and remembers hearing a story about a man who sold his shadow to the devil — the usual Faustian pact. He's fairly sure that's not what's going on here, as his shadow has not disappeared. If anything, it's becoming more present, growing stronger, which is not to say that it's becoming darker. As he walks over the bridge, he tests this and notices: yes, the shadow reacts to light the same way it always has. He just knows somehow that it's getting stronger.

At work, Jon taps his feet under the desk to feel if the shadow's strength is still changing. He expects it to solidify. Or perhaps to accumulate somehow around his feet and ankles, where it is attached to him. Because it is attached to him by the feet, as it always has been. It does feel heavier. But in a way he can't explain. This has nothing to do with feet or ankles.

Alone in the elevator on his way back from lunch, there is a small *whump* sound, which is confusing because it's not the sound of the elevator reaching his destination. It is still travelling. Aware of a cooling sensation, of a certain lightness or cooling of the air around his shoulders and back, he looks behind and sees, or imagines, or believes — afterwards he's not quite sure which — a whole clump of himself which has sheared off from his body and dropped onto the lino, where it is pooling and melting into his shadow like dull grey mercury.

The next day the shadow answers the phone. Jon is finishing a raisin Danish and has pastry flakes in his throat and down his front. He dodges the call, but the shadow does not. No words are spoken (the shadow has no vocal cords), but five minutes later an email arrives from the hated and pernickety Lara Dussman, confirming a contract he hadn't expected to close. Jonathan toasts Shadow with a hazelnut latte and leans back in his chair.

After his shoulders, his hands are the next part of him to feel lighter. He flexes them. His hands do sometimes feel stiff, after typing and texting all day. Or using the Xbox for too long. On those days his fingers feel like bananas thumping on the strings of his guitar. He plays less and less often and this makes him sad.

The day after the Lara Dussman incident, Jon reaches with his right hand for a document from the in-tray and notices that a shadow right hand continues typing. He removes his left hand from the keyboard and watches text continue to appear on the screen. The shadow hands type away without him. Their punctuation is far better than his. Jon reaches for his phone. He scrolls through memes of exotic holiday destinations as the shadow hands work up an overdue report he's been ignoring.

* * *

At dinner, Clare is snippy. She asks if he's alright — he seems different lately. Quiet.

'Huh?'

'You haven't said a word in days. You act like I'm not here.'

'What does that mean?' Jon puts a whole forkful of her risotto into his mouth. 'I'm here aren't I?' He takes a swallow of wine and doesn't meet her eye. He has things on his mind.

'Jonathan!' She slaps her napkin onto the table. Jon has the impression this isn't a new conversation, that they are picking up where they left off on this subject some other time. 'Oh My God,' she says. 'It means... remote. Detached. Silent. Inwardly focussed... In fact — boring.'

Jon scratches his head. Clare's eyes are popping, she's becoming really angry when he finally replies. 'Sorry. I do feel... light.'

'What the fuck does that mean?'

'You tell me! You're the one who says I'm different.'

She takes her plate to the sink, muttering.

'No idea what you're talking about,' he says. But he does know. He and Shadow reached an understanding not two hours earlier. It was as if Shadow understood his deepest feelings. He is full of gratitude. No words necessary.

Jon pushes his chair back and crosses his arms and legs. Clare opens another bottle, clearly upset and near to tears.

'I'm sorry, love.'

He's not looking at her. He's looking at his left foot, dangling. He makes a slight flipping motion and Shadow flips away from him like a coiled towel being flicked in the school showers. Or a carpet being unrolled at speed. Jon stretches out his foot and Shadow is able to reach farther from him than before. Jon opens a beer and drinks in silence. He watches Shadow approach Clare. She is filling the dishwasher and taking quick sips of wine. Jon sees her body stiffen and then relax. The change is very slight and would be imperceptible to someone who didn't know her well. Shadow slowly sniffs her neck and hairline while Jon reaches for his guitar, which hangs on the wall near the table. His left hand folds around the neck and his fingers reach the frets more easily than usual. He strums a couple of chords. Clare drops a glass.

When they go to the bedroom, Jon lounges in her upholstered bedroom chair, one leg slung over the other. He is still drinking his beer, waiting in the half-gloom while Clare is in the bathroom. He takes a drag from a forbidden cigarette. When she opens the bathroom door a beam of yellow light cuts across the bed. Jon is startled and his foot jerks upward. Shadow launches himself forward, encircling Clare's waist. Soon she is smothered in his velvet presence, the two figures becoming indistinguishable. They tip sideways onto the bed. After some frantic movements they slip down onto the sheepskin rug where they remain, rolling back and forth for some time. Eventually Shadow leads her back to the bed. They are silent and, to Jon's relief, apparently joyful.

Jon relaxes into the soft armchair, disinclined to interfere. After a while, he reaches out with his foot and closes the bathroom door.

WHAT MY FATHER LEFT BEHIND
Nathaniel Spain

One of the most horrible items in my father's collection was a mermaid. It ogled him across his desk for seven years, until he died on New Year's Day in 1953.

I was certain it was no more than a fish and a monkey, glued together and surmounted by a wig. Somehow this monstrosity ended up on a stall on Portobello Road, where my father discovered it and presumably fell in love. And so, when he abruptly left this mortal coil, I had to deal with the creature, along with everything else he had shoved into his little townhouse in Pimlico.

The contents rivalled the Hunterian Collection — before it was bombed, anyway. My sisters said they could never return to London after the war, citing incendiary terrors. I thought their horror really lay in the things my father kept in jars. Pig embryos swam in formaldehyde on the kitchen shelves. An eyeball stared from the dining-room sideboard. Before I left for North Africa, the man's interests had been confined to taxidermy, which had been bad enough. I grew up with a boar's head looming over my bed.

It was February by the time the will was read and I received the keys to the townhouse. I remember the day well. London was awash with icy slush. It was dark inside the house — all of the curtains were drawn — and very cold. I managed to scavenge a few lumps of coal for a fire. Then began my attempt to make sense of what Father had left us. The skulls on the dresser, the snakeskins on the wall. It all had to go. My sisters agreed that, in lieu of them providing physical help with the clearance, I could keep two-thirds of any proceeds from sales. I was thereby sufficiently motivated to spend that first day in frenzied industry.

Into the dining room went everything I could reasonably guess the value of. Mostly paintings and antique furniture. Into the study went the bulk of the collection — oddities that were either priceless or worthless. The jars of organs. The pinned insects. Reigning queen of these curios was the mermaid herself. She was a pathetic thing, desiccated and forlornly curled. Her skin was leathery and she wore a pained expression. In some ways, her aspect reminded me of my father. He had been badly burned while on duty as a warden. His face was never quite the same. I locked the study door as I left.

* * *

I slept in my father's bedroom that night. Wind rattled the windowpane. The mattress was ancient, lumpen, and as cold as the floor. The room had a pungent smell — no doubt from the stuffed animal heads which had until recently been mounted on the walls. A long time passed before I fell asleep.

When I woke — or so I thought — it was still dark. The cause of my waking was a portentous click, like a key in a lock.

I could move neither my arms nor my legs, and was overwhelmed by the feeling that something was about to happen. My ears strained intently. At first I could only hear my own breathing. Then there was something more; a kind of rustling or sweeping. Like something being dragged down the hallway. There were no footsteps. I turned my neck with tremendous effort. The door was ajar and through it I could see the corridor beyond. A sliver of moonlight streaked across the wall, painting the floorboards. A shape moved in the shadows, low to the ground. It was drawing towards me.

It's hard to describe the terror of that moment. It was like facing death; knowing that one's life has culminated in this absolute point, and it has all been insufficient. That I could have been better prepared for it, but now the seconds were running out and I must make the most of them.

I watched the shape slither toward the bedroom. There was nothing I could do; I was pinned to the bed like one of the insects in Father's collection. I constructed a fantasy — that it was only a cat or rodent that had got inside a bag and was now stumbling about — but then the shape came into the moonlight. It was the mermaid. Of course it was. Her skeletal arms were outstretched, fixing upon the boards with her ragged nails to haul herself into the bedroom. Her wrinkled face was eyeless, her shrivelled lips gaping wide.

Water, she rasped.

She bumped through the doorway, dragging herself toward the bed. My heart was beating so violently, I thought I might have an attack. I let out a pathetic mumble, eyes bulging from my head. The mermaid inexorably drew beside the bedstead and then out of sight. For a moment I felt relief. At least I was raised up; having no legs, the monstrous creature could do nothing but terrify me.

Water, she rasped again, louder this time. I felt a tugging on the duvet. The fabric strained against my body, rocking me to one side. In a fresh bolt of horror I realised the creature was trying to scale the bedclothes. One claw-like hand strained into view. Then her face, ghoulish and gasping, rose inches from my own.

* * *

When I woke again, the room was in daylight. The sun fell cold and sharp through the window. I started, instinctively throwing the duvet from myself. My limbs were clumsy, and I all but fell from the bed, but at least I could move. I cast around for the mermaid, even looking under the bed, but there was no sign of her.

I peered down the hall. The study door was closed. I padded carefully toward it, the boards cold on my bare feet, and tried the handle. It was still locked. The horror withdrew, replaced by a rush of embarrassment. I hadn't had night terrors for five or six years. Still, the apparition had felt very real. I fetched the keys and unlocked the study.

The mermaid lay as she had before, curled up beside my father's desk. I found I was shaking. I went over and set my hand on her tail, with no small amount of trepidation. It was dry, and rough, and cold. I went to wash my hands, locking the door once again behind me.

* * *

The previous day I had telephoned an antique dealer called Mr Pye, who was due to arrive later that morning. I sat in the parlour and smoked while I waited. My nerves had been restored by two rashers of bacon and a poached egg. I figured the nightmare I'd endured was produced by an excited imagination. It was forgivable to be affected by my return to this house. My father's absence was an open wound, even though we had never been close. And there were fragments of past wounds in the nightmare, too. The most horrible part had been her voice. *Water.* I realised the cigarette had nearly burned my fingers. I swore and stubbed it out.

I was relieved when Mr Pye arrived, for he spared me from the anxiety of thinking. He was a balding man with a large pair of spectacles and a habit of mumbling to himself. I showed him the collection — firstly the inoffensive items in the dining room, which raised only a polite interest, and then those other things locked in the study. He seemed excited. 'Is any of it human?' Pye said, peering into one of the jars.

'One or two, maybe,' I said. 'Are there any — legal issues I should be aware of?'

'I'll look into it.' Pye took off his glasses and wiped them on the hem of his jumper. 'Are you waiting on the opinion of other appraisers, or are you willing to sell today?'

'Depends on your offer.'

Pye let out a giggle and nodded. 'Very well. And what is this?' He gestured toward the mermaid.

I grimaced. 'Horrible, isn't it?'

'Wonderfully horrible. There was a rather fervent trade in them last century. Of course, most were discovered to be fakes.'

'What do you mean, most?'

'Sometimes they couldn't tell one way or the other.' Pye stroked the mermaid's tail. 'We could only be sure if we dissected her, and that would be rather a shame, wouldn't it?'

'I think we can assume it's a fake,' I said.

'On that basis,' Pye replied, 'I might offer thirty pounds.'

'And if it were real?'

'Then we should have to haggle.'

I considered laughing at the man, but then I took pause. It wasn't that I thought the mermaid actually real, any more than last night's ordeal, but if Pye was sufficiently gullible I might be able to squeeze a few more bob out of him. 'How about an X-ray?' I offered. 'That'll show us what's going on inside her, without risking any damage.'

'Jolly good idea,' Pye replied. 'I'll sniff around. See if I can get a university or the like to lend us one.'

Two hours later we had finished negotiating. Pye took the collection; I took a hundred and fifty pounds. Only the mermaid was left. Pye promised to telephone me as soon as he found someone willing to X-ray it. When he had gone, I was left with only the mermaid's company. I wished I'd let him take the bloody thing. I wondered what perversity had led me to do otherwise.

* * *

I went out to buy a pork chop for supper and a bottle of Scotch. I had the cash, after all, and felt the need to steel myself for another night under my father's roof. The cold when I returned was intense. I knocked next door to borrow some coals but nobody was in. I burned some old newspapers and broke down a battered old chair for the fire, for by that point it was late and I didn't know where would be open to sell firewood. I had a smoke while I cooked the chop. The house felt very quiet. It seemed terribly empty, now my father's paraphernalia had gone. With the walls and shelves bare, it was like he had never existed. As if he hadn't been more than his habit. This was a discomfiting thought. I drank two glasses of whisky and braced myself for an early night.

Sleep brought with it a vision of dunes. Hot sand, the taste of it in my mouth. The distant blur of the Atlas Mountains. The skitter of a lizard, the marks it left behind. The shimmer of the sun beating upon the desert, as if it might turn it all to glass.

We rode a Humber alone through the desert. We'd been separated from our company after a sandstorm. There were three of us: myself, Phipps, and a Yorkshireman named Talbot. One of the Humber's two machine guns was broken. We were jumpy; no match for one of Rommel's Tigers.

Then we came across another vehicle. It lay in the lee of a wind-eroded butte and wore a shawl of dust. It looked like a Jeep. Phipps thought it might be a Kübelwagen. There was no sign of movement. Talbot and I got out, Phipps covering us with the machine gun.

When we reached the car, we found a man lying in the shade beside it. His hair was filled with sand and his lips were split, flakes of skin fluttering as he breathed raspingly. He looked up at us beseechingly, eyes crusted. *Wasser*, he said. *Wasser.*

We didn't know how long it would take us to rejoin our company. The Humber was too cramped for a prisoner, even if we wanted another man gulping our water. We talked about shooting him, but none of us felt willing to put a man down like an injured horse. By that point the poor blighter had passed out. So we left him. He was a German, after all.

Water.

I woke to find the mermaid on my chest. Her howling mouth rattled like a stone in a dry gully. Her empty sockets were two additional mouths, straining to swallow me. I screamed. Wrenched myself upright to throw her off.

By the time I was on my feet, she had vanished. I stood, shoulders heaving, duvet hanging from my clenched fist. I was damp with sweat. The floorboards were so cold they stung.

I set the duvet down, listening to the quiet in the house. My breath felt like an intrusion. I walked from my room toward the study. I had locked it before, I was certain, but when I turned the handle it clicked open. I inched my head through the doorway and peered inside.

The mermaid was lying under a pall of moonlight. She was curled as always, her hands half-covering her withered face. A lonely object in an empty room. Then she withdrew her hands and looked at me.

I closed the door. I scratched my arm, digging my fingernails in hard enough to leave welts. The pain felt real enough. I inhaled, bracing myself, then opened the door once again. I met a wave of water. A deep, black, rushing torrent of salt and muck and icy chill. It knocked the air from me.

I appeared to be underwater, surrounded by endless fathoms and drifting motes of algae. Moonlight scythed from an unreachable surface. It was so cold that it burned. I floundered, feeling the weight of the water on all sides. Bubbles erupted from my throat. I turned, kicking my legs, falling beyond terror into some unknown emotional plane.

There was a shadow in the water below me. It was barely discernible against the gloom of those deeper places. At first I thought it was the mermaid, here to pursue me in her own element, but no — it was a human form. All four limbs were motionless, allowing the figure to be born down, deeper and darker, until it would become inseparable from the surrounding murk.

I found myself swimming toward it. I willed myself through the cold, body sluggish, clothes like lead. As hard as I swam, I could not reach the figure. I was suddenly overwhelmed by the feeling that this was my father. And he was sinking out of sight. The shock of that, the love and fear and misery of it, was more excruciating than the water pressure. I opened my mouth to call to him and the ocean rushed in.

* * *

I spluttered. A cold wind grasped at me. I blinked water from my eyes. Rain was falling on the streets of London. I had never sleepwalked before, and it took several moments for me to gather what was happening. I was standing outside my father's house in only my pyjamas. It was very dark. Nobody else was on the street. The rain was washing the icy slush away, guttering and choking into the roadside drains.

I stepped back toward the house. The door yawned expectantly. I paused before I reached it and looked upward. The window of my father's study looked upon the street. A lamp had cast a sliver of light against the glass, and with that illumination I saw the mermaid sitting within. She was perfectly still, gazing with her head tilted upward. She did not appear to see me. I wondered what she was looking at. Then I realised it was the rain itself, dripping down the windowpanes.

* * *

At ten o'clock the following morning, my sister Eleanor telephoned me. I answered with a wince. I had drunk most of the remaining Scotch when I got back in, and with this heavy sedative had fallen asleep in the sitting-room armchair. My head was feeling delicate.

'How are you, Charlie?' her voice sang down the line. 'Is everything alright?'

'It's — well,' I managed. 'I've cleared the house. Got a few bob out of it, too.'

'Good for you. Thanks again, Charlie. You know how much Penny and I detest London.'

'Yes.'

'I called her just before I rang you,' she continued. 'We're wondering how we'll manage the property. We thought it might be best to sell it, but as you've only been renting since — well, perhaps you would like to live there? You can buy our share once you're on your feet.'

'No no,' I said mildly. 'We can sell it. I'm not that fond of London either.'

'Oh really? Well, very good. We'll proceed as planned.'

'Eleanor —'

'Hmm?'

'Do you think Dad got all of that bric-a-brac because he felt lonely? With all of us gone, I mean. Something to — occupy him.'

There followed a pause. 'I hadn't really considered it,' Eleanor replied. 'He always had the stuffed animals, didn't he?

On that note — you didn't happen to keep that little ermine from mine and Penny's room, did you?'

'I'm afraid not. But I can give Pye a ring if you wanted it.'

'Oh no, that's quite alright. Probably best to let it go.'

We said our goodbyes. I put the receiver down, feeling slightly dazed. I finished my cup of tea then went upstairs. I took one of my father's coats out of his wardrobe — the largest one, well-worn with patches on the elbows and a hundred buttons and pockets. I found half a dozen oddities inside — his old pipe, a notebook filled with indecipherable scribbles, a few pages torn from a magazine, and a little wooden creature which was either a lion or a goat or something else entirely. I put each of them reverently on the bedside table. Then I went to the study.

The mermaid was by the window, still entranced by the residual drops of last night's rain. I walked across to her. She did not move; there was no sign that she was anything but a grotesque model. When I touched her tail she was as dry and lifeless as ever.

Carefully, I wrapped the coat around her. I thought it might not cover her, but I needn't have worried, and with this veil I lifted her into my arms like a child. She was paper-light.

I carried her out of the townhouse, locking it behind me. I didn't attempt to take the bus or Tube or hail a cab; I walked the streets I had run down as a boy. I meandered through neighbourhoods, passing families and workers and all the hustle and bustle of thousands of lives trying to make something of what time they had while life was relatively good. Some of the streets still bore the marks of bombing, the gaunt shells of one-time homes, the piles of rubble.

I walked toward the Thames. The river cut a grey swathe through the city. Battersea Power Station rose stark upon the far bank, breathing plumes of smoke into the pale sky.

I cradled the mermaid as I walked to the river's edge. A strand of hair had escaped the coat. It fluttered in the air. I clambered down the embankment, easing myself beside the opaque currents, and knelt in the mud. I lowered the coat to the water and opened it, allowing the mermaid to slide into the river.

There was a silvery flash, a full-bodied flick, and then she was gone.

THE END OF
THE WORLD
Flo Ward

On Tuesday the sun doesn't set.

We're sitting outside Scotti's, Gus holding onto his empty foam-rimmed pint glass, and me still nursing an inch of house white. The light is golden, full bodied, early May, glinting on the glass exterior of the building opposite. The sun makes strands of Gus's otherwise dark hair amber. I'm swirling the wine around the bottom of my glass without drinking it, because I don't want the moment to end. I've always been like this, pleading one more drink, one more song, five more minutes in bed in the morning when the sheets are heavy and the temperature is exactly right. Gus is always moving forward, always awake and purposeful, while I try to keep things still long enough to be certain I've made the most of them. One more kiss before we brush our teeth, one more moment before lights out, please.

Not just yet, I say when he unhooks his coat from the back of the chair. Gus humours me in these situations, says something about how the next moment we have will be just as nice as this one, and I envy his trust in the future. Gus has rainy day savings, performs household chores with enough regularity that he is always pre-empting dirt and untidiness, but lets the dust settle after an argument. I find it hard to believe in what isn't in front of me, and become anxious after any imperfect interaction. Neither of us predicts what is going to happen, of course.

We don't realise that the sun hasn't set, because our news notifications aren't turned on. Who was the first person to notice, I wonder later, imagining a startled meteorologist, the alarm travelling down an unseen chain to the newsroom, a flurry of text messages sent from journalists to their families and friends, reality spreading outwards like something spilled until it touches us.

When the news does touch us we are still outside Scotti's, me still making a meal of my wine with tiny, holy sips. Gus leans back on his chair, his eyes closed and a hand on my knee in absent affection. It's seven minutes late, apparently, someone says at a table near us — the kind of contextless overheard snippet of conversation that wouldn't have meant anything if it hadn't coincided with Gus receiving a message with a link to the breaking news article.

So that's how it begins. It's curious at first, mainly the sensation of seeing the headline and hearing it being discussed around us at the same time: we're in the middle of something. I'm reminded of how when the queen died I was sitting in the National Gallery toilet scrolling through the news on my phone, and I heard a gasp over the sound of running water from the woman at the sink outside the cubicle door. I've told that story several times since.

A man at the table next to us shows us something on his phone, and Gus bends over to look. Weird, isn't it, I say to his companion, as if I know her, and she agrees it is. I can hear the man telling Gus that it's probably the result of some kind of nuclear explosion, that Russia is involved, and Gus is responding with diplomatic sounds of agreement (ever patient), glancing up to catch my eye and grin. I take out my phone and message our group chat, *should we all be panicking?* with a sunshine emoji, to which someone replies with a series of question marks and someone else writes, *lol just looked this up.* I feel a bizarre kind of pride at this ambivalence. All these people in a frenzy but not us! Where were we when the world ended? Just having a drink! Just watching *Gossip Girl*!

Eventually the woman interrupts her friend's explanation of a global cover-up to say that they need to leave. We each say goodbye, in an awkward way that suggests more kinship than we have with these strangers, and the woman wishes us good luck. I feel uneasy at that, and tell Gus I think they're both nut jobs when we're out of earshot.

The city is out of sync. It's a glistening, glossy light that illuminates everything in a warm yolk-yellow, so that the pavement seems to breathe and the gutter glints with yesterday's rain and leaves, trodden into sludge. The silver inside of a discarded crisp packet reflects the sun. But it is also strangely busy, people amassing at the entrance of the Tube station as if commuting to or from work, although it's nearly nine pm. Not everyone moves with a sense of purpose. A woman stands in the middle of the street looking at the sky, a bewildered expression on her face. Elsewhere there is a bag of groceries abandoned. I say, look, we could forage our dinner, but Gus doesn't find this as amusing as I do.

We decide to walk to Gus's flat, which neither of us have done from here before (it will take two hours), but the Tube is busy and the light is, at least, very nice. We still haven't eaten dinner. The excitement of the situation distracts me from being hungry, until we pass a sandwich shop, still open. I say we should go in. We've timed this perfectly, actually, Gus notes.

(This is our thing: to keep discussing and affirming our good fortune as if we've made canny decisions — good thing we saved that last episode so we could watch it on a rainy Sunday; wise of us to book our flight for the day *before* rail strikes; smart that we didn't go to the cinema tonight or we'd be oblivious to all this, stumbling out of the film into the light with our body clocks thrown off.)

The man behind the counter piles a sliced baguette with folded ham and a tangle of rocket and tells us that normally he'd be shut by now, but why not cash in on a few more hours of business? There's a TV in the corner of the room showing a meteorologist being interviewed about historic freak weather events. The news anchor says it is one of over eleven instances of erratic weather we've seen in the last fifteen years, and he interrupts her to say it is unprecedented. I go on Instagram and click through a barrage of stories: infographics on global warming, Russian nuclear attacks, something about crop failure and rising migration, a selfie with the hashtag *#eternalgoldenhour*.

Do you think we'll go to work tomorrow? I ask, and this is somehow absurdly funny. Why shouldn't we? But also, how could we?

When we get to the river we sit on a bench and I call Mum, who swings between hysteria and uncharacteristic resignation about the whole thing. There are only a couple of tins of tomatoes in the cupboard, she says, it will barely last until Thursday lunchtime. Gus reads all the messages he's received and interrupts my conversation to confirm it's a global phenomenon, not currently considered dangerous, still unexplained. Mum tells me I should try and get the train home this evening and I tell her that's an overreaction, and what would I do at home anyway? The sun isn't going to set any sooner over Reading. I feel a little guilty after hanging up, for being so dismissive. Gus and I sit in silence on the bench and watch a woman engaged in a frantic phone conversation a few steps away from us. I can't travel with the kids, she is saying. It's not realistic.

We walked down this stretch of river on one of our early dates two years ago, and Gus told me about the mudlarks who fished jewellery and gold teeth from its banks. That was back when it was common practice to tip corpses into the water, the river full of bodies and their treasure rather than bits of plastic packaging and polystyrene cups. Although of course, Gus said then, there are still plenty of ancient bones in there, and we peered into the river's depths, awed by the way this great murky vein of history coursed through the city. These kinds of stories are typical of Gus, who loves to know about the histories of innocuous street signs and places where buildings once stood, who told me early on that what thrilled him most about the world was how it was constantly changing. This is our major philosophical difference — I fear the steady march of time — but it didn't stop me falling in love with him.

Shall we get going? Gus asks eventually, as if we have somewhere to be. We keep the river on our left, heading east, not looking at the map. Gus doesn't say much. I point things out to him as we walk, trying to draw him back to me when it feels like he's drifting elsewhere. Look at the surface of the river in the light, at how strangely solid it seems, how gently rippled. Look at that bus, do you think the driver just left it there? Look at those children, it's gone eleven and they're running about with their book bags. Look at the colour of the sky, it's so beautiful.

Gus's street is quiet and most of the houses have drawn their curtains. We agree it's eerie, but it takes me a moment to realise that this is because the sound of traffic has lessened, that the steady swoosh is now almost indiscernible. Have people gone to bed, or have they left? Gus takes his house keys out as I step over a pigeon minced into the road.

* * *

Shall we have a cup of tea? Gus asks, standing inside the kitchen holding the kettle aloft. Or coffee? Or wine?

Coffee, I say, turning the radio on. We listen to a report from Sydney, where it's nine am and still dark and people are queueing to get into the airport. I try, and fail, to remember the name of a girl I knew at university who moved to Melbourne. The stovetop coffee pot sputters and bubbles over, coffee dribbling onto the hob with a hiss. Gus shows me an article on his phone: a car has melted in Arizona's unrelenting midday heat.

We stayed up all night like this once before, sipping tea and putting the world to rights. It wasn't long after we met, the early stage of a relationship when time spent together is still like throwing a rope and hoping they are there to catch it, when saying *we could do this* is letting it take your weight and praying that you're still attached. So you start small with *let's try that new place for a drink* and *we should see that film,* and then *I'd like to go travelling one day* becomes *we should go travelling together* and *I want to live north of the river* becomes *we'll live north of the river* and the future comes into focus, sharpened by two wills pointed in the same direction. That's how it had been last time we sat in this kitchen at four in the morning, giddy on mint tea and talk of the rest of our lives.

Now we drink our coffee in mostly silence, listening to everything unfolding elsewhere, noticing how the light falls over the plants on the windowsill, rich and warm and life-giving. Gus puts his arms around me and I lean back into him, eyes closed, and wonder how long the sun can hold its hot breath on my face.

ABOUT THE CONTRIBUTORS

Eva Carson was born in Glasgow in 1984 and now lives in Fife. She's inspired by the spooky and the strange, towns and cities, and stories of the coast. Her stories have been published by The Fiction Desk, *Carmen et Error*, and *404 Ink Magazine*.

Her website is evacarson.com

Jack Edwards aims to write down-to-earth stories about everyday people, but finds that a twist of horror tends to creep in through the cracks. He grew up in a sleepy East Anglian village before moving to Edinburgh, and is currently finalising a novel about the perils of leaving your hometown in the search for something better.

David Frankel's short stories have been shortlisted in numerous competitions including The Commonwealth Prize, The Bristol Prize, The Bridport Prize, The Society of Authors' ALCS Tom-Gallon Trust Award, and the Fish Memoir Prize.

His work has been widely published in journals and anthologies and as chapbooks by Nightjar Press and Salo Press. His short story collection, *Forgetting is How We Survive*, was shortlisted for the 2024 Edge Hill Prize.

His website is davidfrankel.co.uk.

Tamsin Hopkins writes poetry and fiction. Her short fiction collection *SHORE TO SHORE, River Stories* (Cinnamon Press) employs the mythology of individual rivers around the world to illustrate the interconnectedness between humans and living rivers. It was shortlisted for the Rubery Prize and longlisted for the Edge Hill Prize.

A previous winner of the Aesthetica Prize, her writing has appeared in many magazines and anthologies including *New Ghost Stories II* by The Fiction Desk.

Rob Redman founded The Fiction Desk in 2010 and has been editing and publishing short stories ever since. He's the editorial director and co-founder of Uncertain Stories.

Lucy Scott is an artist and animator, and has exhibited her work in Edinburgh, Manchester, London, Dublin, Tiblisi, and New York. She's the art director and co-founder of Uncertain Stories.

Nathaniel Spain is a writer and designer based in the North East of England. His writing has featured in *Ten Poets Get to the Bottom of Some Grisly Crimes* (Sidekick Books, 2024), *Unfurl* (The Braag, 2023), and journals including *Hare's Paw*, *Carmina Magazine*, and others. He has a background in publishing, environmentalism, and the community sector, and is the editor of Carnyx Press.

His website is www.nathanielspain.co.uk.

Mark Taylor is a writer and learning technologist based in Manchester.

He publishes daily microfiction at markiswrit.ing.

Flo Ward is a writer from London. She is currently working on her first novel, exploring friendship and obsession in the digital world.

UNCERTAIN STORIES

Uncertain Stories was founded in 2025 to publish new short fiction with a supernatural or speculative edge. For more information about our anthologies and other titles, see our website:

www.uncertainstories.com